A Special Storm

A Dora Ellison Mystery

Book 5

A Special Storm

A Dora Ellison Mystery

Book 5

First Edition

By David E. Feldman

For Matt, Michele, and Zoe

Table of Contents

Cast of Characters

Many characters are recurring, though not all recur in all the books. Their lives, triumphs, and defeats sometimes occur over the course of multiple books.

Dora Ellison: My heroine, a sweet, sensitive yet violent martial arts savant who finds herself a reluctant detective in *Not Today*, Book 1. Traumatized as a child, her story can be found in the prequel, *Storm Warnings*.

Lt. Francesca "Franny" Hart: Dora's love interest in *Not Today*, Book 1.

Missy Winters: Dora's investigator partner and love interest from *A Gathering Storm*, Book 2, onward.

Adam Geller: The owner of Geller Investigations. In his sixties, he has multiple health conditions, which keep him from more actively investigating and explain why he needs Dora and Missy to work under the umbrella of his license.

Thelma: Adam's often sarcastic office manager who possesses a dry, caustic wit.

Charlie Bernelli Jr: The outspoken owner of the Bernelli Group, a local ad agency, and friend of Dora and Missy's. An alcoholic who is sometimes in recovery, often not.

Christine Pearsall-Bernelli: Charlie's love interest and eventual wife. The city clerk in *Not Today*, Book 1, and the mayor of Beach City from *A Gathering Storm*, Book 2, onward. An observant Catholic with a politically conservative point of view.

C3: Charlie Bernelli Jr.'s son, aka Charlie Bernelli III. He struggles with an ongoing drug problem and is sometimes in recovery, sometimes not.

Depending on his degree of sobriety, he works as a cab driver or drug counselor. In a long-term relationship with Sarah Turner, which produces daughter, Livvie.

Tom Volkov: Owner/editor of *The Beach City Chronicle* in *Not Today*, Book 1.

Sarah Turner: Writer/reporter for *The Beach City Chronicle* in *Not Today*, Book 1, and editor/owner from *A Gathering Storm*, Book 2, onward. In a long-term relationship with C3, which produces daughter, Livvie.

Vanessa Burrell: Wife of Jesse Burrell and sister-in-law of Agatha and Rudy Raines. Mother of Drew and Buster.

Agatha Raines: A Beach City councilwoman. Married to Rudy.

Rudy Raines: Owner of Rudy's, a restaurant/bar. Married to Agatha.

Paul Ganderson: A police detective. Half of "the Goose and the Gander" detective team. Known for his cheap suits, slicked-back hair, acne, and blunt style.

Gerald Mallard: A police detective. The other half of "the Goose and the Gander" detective team. Known for his folksy style, ridiculously expensive clothes, and alcoholic/demanding wife, Kay.

Catherine Trask: Police lieutenant at the BCPD. Has a tempestuous relationship with Detective Paul Ganderson.

Carolyn Trask: Sister of Catherine. Works at Cobb's Diner, which becomes Mae's Diner after *Not Today*, Book 1.

Terry Stalwell: Police chief for the BCPD. A good, fair man.

George Cobb: Police captain for the BCPD in *Not Today*, Book 1. Known for his cruelty.

Horace Cobb: Owner of Cobb's Diner in *Not Today*, Book 1.

Chapter 1

The Montgomery School's auditorium was a collection of noisy children, chatting parents, motorized wheelchairs, and gurneys carrying young people connected to breathing tubes and monitors, along with support staff and medical personnel nearly as numerous as their charges.

Onstage, the special stars of the moment were already singing their hearts out to the accompaniment of a piano played by a young woman in front of the stage. The music was a potpourri of inspirational, can-do, and ability-friendly songs.

As they entered the hall and looked around for seats, C3 brushed back his blond hair and settled one-year-old Olivia against his chest in the blue baby carrier while Sarah, her dark ponytail tied back and dressed, as usual, all in black, hefted a bag of supplies. His name was C3 because his father was Charlie Bernelli Junior and he was Charlie III, aka C3. Their friend Vanessa, petite and pretty with dark-golden skin and shoulder-length dreads, carried silent Buster, now nearly two-and-a-half, along with an overstuffed plaid baby bag, while six-year-old Drew tagged along beside her.

The two families were late and had to find seats near the rear of the auditorium. After several minutes, all six were as settled as any families with young children, special or not, could be.

C3 and Sarah had known by Sarah's second month of pregnancy that Olivia, or Livvie, as they called her, would be a child with Down syndrome and were prepared to welcome her to the world long before her birth. Part of their preparation had been to engage with the local special-needs community, meet a few other parents, and join both in-person and online organizations and parent groups. Upon Livvie's birth, they had instantly fallen in love with their special daughter and were determined to pave her way in life as best they could.

Before their current situation, C3 had never paid much attention to people with special needs; to him, they were people and they had special needs, but beyond that, they didn't much enter his awareness. But that had changed. He'd grown aware, and then vigilant, then compassionate. He looked around the auditorium, and while many special people were facing the stage, quite a few were engaging with their families, with each other, or with their own inner worlds. His eyes traveled from one special child to the next, and what he saw wasn't people who were less, but people who were more. What they lacked wasn't ability, but anger, hate, bigotry, resentment, hostility, and rage. They weren't focused on getting ahead by any means possible, including—perhaps especially— by trampling their fellow humans. They weren't particularly focused on getting ahead at all. They simply did the best they could at whatever was at hand. There was no competition; there was life, and while there was pain and difficulty, there was also love.

C3 smiled and looked at Sarah, who smiled back. Livvie was already making them better people, helping them transcend their challenges and their egos.

He watched a middle-aged woman with boxy black hair, red lipstick, and clenched features walk up the aisle from the front of the auditorium, deep in conversation with another well-dressed woman who had the of- ficial look of an administrator. The second woman was doing her best to placate the woman with the clenched features, but the latter gesticulated emphatically, and her voice rose above the music.

"Don't you dare tell me what's best for my Stuart! You refuse to return my calls, and now you brush me off by saying you know best? How dare you!" The pair disappeared through the doors at the rear of the auditorium. Moments later, the administrator returned, alone.

The vignette reminded C3 of how he and Sarah would have to advocate for Livvie. Off in the distance was the vague yet looming notion that she would probably require care and advocacy after he and Sarah were gone. *What would that look like?* he wondered. He pushed the thought away and returned his attention to the auditorium, and the music and song emanating from the stage. He allowed his environment to wash over him, sublimating his thoughts and fears. He reached for his daughter's tiny hand and rubbed her wrist between his fingers. She turned to him and smiled, and his heart melted.

C3 and Sarah had made a point of including Vanessa Burrell in their Livvie-related plans as often as they could. Vanessa was struggling; she'd faced one challenge after another, from her beloved husband Jesse's murder to her relationship with Lorne, who'd been abusive. Recently, her second-born son—two-and-a-half-year-old Buster, who'd been a chattering, inquisitive, highly intelligent toddler—had grown silent and disinterested. He rarely responded to any stimulus, even to the adoration and increasingly frantic-yet-loving interventions of Vanessa, his single mother. Drew, his older brother, had been bewildered by the change in his younger sibling but was soon distracted by the world around him and the new universe of kindergarten.

The chorus of special people on the stage swelled and crescendoed, and one young man's voice soared above the rest. The male singers traded call-and-response lyrics with the female singers, followed by a chorus sung by the entire company.

C3, Sarah, and much of the audience were lifted emotionally and carried along by the music. Many in the audience sang along as feelings of unity, shared experience, and love permeated the crowd.

C3 watched Buster with curiosity, noting his wide-eyed, vacant look. The toddler appeared unaware of the music or the audience hubbub. He sat on his mother's knee, her arm protectively around his chest; he seemed indifferent to her and to anything else.

C3's attention was drawn to another woman standing just inside the door to the lobby. The woman was thin, with sunken eyes, a bony face, and stringy dark-blonde hair. She wore tight black pants and a red collared shirt that was open below her veined neck and hung loosely at her waist.

The woman's eyes were flat, her expression empty—devoid of feeling. She appeared to neither have compassion for nor be engaged with the event. She was apart, aloof, and watching, as though the part of her brain that felt emotions had been entirely removed.

C3 instinctively wrapped his arms around Livvie, clutched her to him, and gave her a wet kiss on the cheek. She turned to him, her face lit with happy surprise.

He overheard Sarah talking to Vanessa and gesturing toward the woman. "That's Diana Moran in the crimson blouse and black pants. She's not a parent. I've seen her with some of the NIMBY crowd."

"NIMBY crowd?" Vanessa asked.

"People who don't want the school in their backyards, so to speak. Not in my backyard—NIMBY."

Vanessa sounded surprised. "They don't want a school for special-needs kids in the area? Why not?"

"All I can tell you is," Sarah explained, "people from that crowd write letter after letter to *The Chronicle*. They're furious that Montgomery kids are anywhere near their homes."

"What, they think autism is contagious?"

C3 glanced at his girlfriend, and Sarah returned his look. The subject wasn't new to them.

"You'd be surprised by what some people think about autism," Sarah said.

"Yeah, I would be," Vanessa declared.

"It's fear," C3 interjected. "They have no facts, and rather than investigate for themselves, they make crap up to keep their fear at bay. Or they get what passes for information from internet forums."

The blonde woman was leaning against the wall, opposite the windows, her arms folded across her chest as she surveyed the room. Her face was the papery brown of someone who'd been in the sun too often and for too many years; her eyes met C3's. He refused to look away. She gave him an ugly smile.

He turned his attention to the performers, and the part of his mind that worried for his daughter took note of each special young person's physical or developmental challenges while marveling at their earnest displays of talent. During the troupe's performance of "My Girl," one of the young women—a girl with red hair and a wide mouth, who wore a forest-green skirt and a sun-yellow blouse—drifted from her spot on one side of the stage. She walked solemnly to centerstage and took the hand of a bony young man with brown hair that fell in long bangs over his eyes, which were heavy-lidded with long eyelashes. The young man was shuffling in place, his feet turned inward, his free hand flapping in a way that indicated he had cerebral palsy.

C3 looked to see what Diana Moran might think of the performances, but the woman had disappeared.

The shuffling young man's face was upturned and serene as the other voices fell away and the piano struck a simple chord. Then the young man began to sing a new piece. He sang with such feeling, such gentle compassion, tenderness, and love, that C3 and Sarah exchanged a look of astonishment. Vanessa gasped. The auditorium fell silent except for a few spartan piano chords and the young man's clarion vocal, as he sang the aria "Che Gelida Manina," from Puccini's opera *La bohème,* his astonishing voice sliding effortlessly between a strong, clear tenor and a honeyed falsetto.

C3 couldn't help but notice an enormous, burly young man with light-blond hair and an overbite in the back row of the singers, all of whom but he were focused on the piano player-conductor, who was offering cues by mouthing the lyrics to each song. The massive young man appeared fascinated with the two hand-holding young people in the front row of singers.

As the young man with cerebral palsy sang, the other performers were coaxed to the wings by young women in black, who did their best to remain unobtrusive, leaving the gifted young man with the clear voice alone on the stage.

"Wow. He can saaang!" Vanessa was awestruck.

"That's Julian Lockhart," Sarah explained. "He's kind of a vocal prodigy. Sings at every Montgomery event."

As Julian approached the song's final notes, a perfectly coiffed man of eighty in a three-piece suit, who'd been seated in the front row, ascended a short flight of stairs to the stage, helped by a middle-aged woman with dyed 1950s-style blonde hair. She supported his right arm with both of her hands, and he carried a wooden plaque bearing a gold plate.

"That's Mason Montgomery—the school's founder," Sarah whispered. "With him is Sharon Hurley, his office manager and hatchet woman. Do not cross that woman." Sarah was emphatic. "She's vicious and holds a grudge forever."

"Noted," Vanessa responded.

The facility's founder and his assistant moved to centerstage just as Julian's voice rose on one of the song's several climax notes. The English translation of the lyrics was, "How do I live? I survive!" As he sang the final note of the phrase, Julian took a breath and was about to continue when a crack like a branch breaking sounded from outside one of the auditorium's windows.

Faces turned toward the sound, but C3 was fixated on Julian Lockhart. The song's next note was a gurgle in the young man's throat, as a maroon dot appeared on his Adam's apple, followed by a spurting fountain of dark-red blood, staining his white shirt a plum color as he folded to the floor.

Screams filled the auditorium. Pandemonium ensued.

A man of about seventy, dressed in blue jeans and a white shirt, his gray hair brushed back and falling to his shoulders, ran to the stage and knelt beside the young singer. He cradled Julian's head in his arms and sobbed.

Next to the fallen singer, Mason Montgomery stood still and looked confused. One side of his jacket and face were covered in blood. He slowly removed a white handkerchief from the front pocket of his jacket with a shaking hand and, grimacing, tried to wipe it away.

Moments later, sirens could be heard over the crying and wailing of attendees as more than a dozen police officers and several EMT units arrived. While people held one another, draped themselves over loves ones' bodies, or cringed on the floor, the police quickly assessed the scene and blocked the exits, both from the auditorium and the building. Officers were stationed at the doors, while others rushed to the area outside the window, which had been broken by the gun shot. EMT personnel tended to the young victim, but they were too late.

The police ordered everyone to lie on the floor and freeze in place while they searched for an active shooter. Once security at the doors was established, officers walked among the performers on stage, the staff, administrators, and the audience. A yellow marker was placed at the feet of the victim, and a single avenue of passage was established from the auditorium to the cafeteria.

Everyone was then herded along that avenue. As they walked along the hallway, C3 could see through windows that the entire perimeter of the school had been cordoned off with yellow police tape. The hallway echoed with crying children, the mechanical whir of motorized wheelchairs, and the squeak of gurney wheels.

The cafeteria tables and chairs that had occupied the front of the room were moved off to the side by caregivers, aides, and janitorial staff to make room for the gurneys and wheelchairs.

As the scene unfolded, C3 had dragged Sarah to the floor and clutched Livvie to his chest. Sarah pressed herself to Livvie's back, so she was sandwiched between them.

Vanessa had also pulled her boys to the floor, as had many other parents with loved ones who were not strapped into chairs and connected to machines. Vanessa held both her boys close and she and Sarah locked eyes through the entire terrifying experience, their gazes communicating shock and horror and comfort.

For C3, Sarah and Vanessa, the experience and the fact that their children were with them would remain a wound for the rest of their lives.

• • •

An hour later, C3, Sarah, Vanessa, and the three children were huddled together in the school's cafeteria—the three adults forming a circle, their arms around one another's shoulders, the two boys sheltered between them.Once the screaming began, Drew's body stiffened—grew rigid—and he screamed into his mother's shirt, soaking it with tears. He continued clinging to her legs with both fists. Both he and Livvie would have nightmares and night terrors for months. All three of the parents would go on to struggle with intrusive thoughts and dreams, as the horror they witnessed remained with each of them in unique and different ways.

Buster remained expressionless throughout.

Sarah and Vanessa pressed their foreheads together and cried, their eyes wide with shock and horror. The sight of Julian Lockhart's throat spurting blood, and the sound of his beautiful voice being reduced to a strangled gurgle would stay with them both forever.

Sarah would later remember being grateful for her daughter's presence. Her responsibility as a mother forced her mind into the moment and away from her own terror. Mommy mode took over. Livvie slept in her carrier, pressed to her father's chest, having fallen asleep just before the shooting. Sarah caressed the top of her daughter's head, stroking her hair, and whispering quiet words of comfort.

In contrast to the hubbub before and during the show, the crowded cafeteria was hushed and nearly silent. Families and friends coalesced, whispering quietly and, for the moment, patiently.

C3 was struggling with an avalanche of anxiety. He was saying the word *surrender* to himself over and over while focusing on the deep abdominal breathing exercises he practiced when he meditated. His Narcotics Anonymous sponsor had directed him to meditate daily, but he found the practice confusing and challenging, and he thought himself a failure at it. So he relegated his meditation to perhaps once every two weeks.

Vanessa continued praying out loud, asking Jesus to "keep us all safe," while clutching both her sons.

Sarah, who, as editor and owner of *The Chronicle,* was used to running her mini media empire, began issuing instructions—mainly to "stay low," "be careful," "speak quietly," and "keep walking," depending on the circumstance. She went from Mommy mode to editor mode, and alternated between taking video of the shooting's aftermath, recording everything she saw into the voice memo app on her phone, and interviewing the few people she could find who were willing to talk. The police quickly intervened, asking her not to interview people until they did so first. Sarah wasn't happy about this, but she did as she was asked.

Claire Sumner, the Montgomery School's principal, announced that all school events would be suspended until further notice and that people would be allowed to leave the building once they were interviewed by the police.

Officers were assigned to accompany anyone needing a bathroom. The teacher's lounge was designated a "privacy area," where diapers and clothing could be changed and the medical needs of special children and adults attended to. Pizzas from the cafeteria's storage refrigerators were heated and distributed, along with juice and apple sauce.

C3, Sarah, and Vanessa gave a police officer descriptions of everything they'd seen and heard at the crime scene before, during, and immediately following the shooting.

"I saw someone at one of the windows—about a third of the way back from the stage," C3 said. "But I couldn't see the person's face, and I couldn't tell you what they were wearing. Just a flash of brown, really. I'm not even sure if it was a man or a woman. And metal—maybe a rifle barrel with a scope."

"I didn't see anything," Vanessa offered. "It happened too fast. There was a firecracker sound, and the singer was suddenly bleeding and fell. That was it. At that point, I was taking care of my boys."

All around them, children were crying, asking questions, or gazing around in bewilderment. Adults in the room were nearly as confused. Sarah had already called Lemieux, her associate editor, who would write the story of the day's events and post them to *The Chronicle*'s website while Esther, her assistant and Internet guru, posted to social media.

Chapter 2

In a small strip mall in the center of Beach City, on Long Island's south shore, was a storefront that housed Geller Investigations. The storefront was divided into the front, a reception area comprised of a desk, an office chair behind the desk, another chair opposite the desk that was for clients, and two others off to the side and next to an end table that offered old issues of *People, Cosmopolitan,* and *Men's Health* magazines. The end table and two chairs served as a waiting area. On the wall behind the office chair was the framed professional license of Adam Geller.

Adam was sitting in the client chair facing the desk. He was sixty-five years old and five feet eight inches tall, with gray hair and a matching mustache and goatee. He'd once been an athlete, and despite those days being long gone, he retained a surprising degree of muscle and strength.

He'd just finished telling Thelma—his office manager, occasional confidant, and constant critic, who was sitting in the office chair—about an unpleasant medical procedure he'd endured at a major New York City cancer hospital.

"What made the whole damned thing even worse was that it was performed by eleven-year-old girls."

"Eleven? Stop exaggerating." Thelma's honking tone might as well have been calling to someone several blocks away. She was dressed in a gray sweater over a white button-down blouse whose collars were flipped over the sweater's neck. Her hair was battleship gray streaked with white and stood straight up, like the bride of Frankenstein's. Her eyes were small and sharp, and her lips pressed tightly together in a permanent expression of displeasure.

"Well, maybe they were thirteen," Adam grudgingly offered.

Thelma made a clucking sound with her tongue and looked away. "I suspect they had medical degrees."

Adam shook his head and waggled a finger. "To do what they did to me wouldn't require a medical license—a porn license, maybe."

"It's always something with you."

"Death is nonexistence," Adam recited in a monotone. "It'll be the same experience after I'm gone as it was before I was here."

"Ugh." Thelma rolled her eyes. "This again!"

Adam looked back at her. "Seneca—Roman philosopher."

Thelma's eyes looked back steadily. "Self-pity," she said emphatically. "My boss."

A woman's voice called from the other side of the wall dividing the front and back of the store space.

"Seneca was born in Spain!"

Adam brightened. "She's right. He moved to Rome later."

On the other side of the wall, two women were sitting together at one of two desks and looking into a laptop computer. The walls were bare except for a hanging calendar and a printed list of clients' names and addresses, along with short descriptions of the work to be performed for each.

Dora Ellison had a pale, pinkish complexion and was five feet eight inches tall and just shy of one hundred and fifty pounds, nearly all of it muscle. Her dark wavy hair fell over the collar of her T-shirt, which read "Shay's Mixed Martial Arts," a place she frequented and occasionally taught. Beside her was Missy Winters, who was a half foot shorter and significantly rounder and softer.

"I think we have all the pictures we need," Dora advised.

Missy sat back and bit her upper lip, squinting at the grainy nighttime photos, the first few of which showed the estranged wife of one of Geller's clients entering her apartment building with a short man in a sport jacket, collared shirt, and slacks. The man wore enormous glasses with thick frames; something about his bearing suggested opulence. The client's wife wore a dark dress that clung to her body while she clung to the opulent man's arm. The date and time stamp were from the previous Saturday night, just prior to midnight. The next few photos were awash in the bright sunshine of eleven thirty the following morning and revealed the same couple—he in the same clothes as the night before, she in slacks and a short-sleeved blouse—exiting her building.

The photos were saved in a directory on a server that all of the office computers could access. The directory's label read "Maverick Lockhart," the name of the client who'd hired Geller Investigations to investigate and document the affair his estranged wife, Emily, was having.

Missy glanced at Dora, who nodded assent, then sent the photo's links to Adam for his approval.

"What I don't understand," Dora said, picking up on a thread from their earlier conversation, "is why we weren't invited in the first place. Sarah and C3 are friends. We love Olivia. And I've been sitting for Nessa's boys for more than a year."

Missy looked mildly surprised. "Dor, a boy was murdered there! Why do you care that we weren't invited?" Her dark-beige skin wrinkled between her eyebrows.

A corner of Dora's mouth twisted. "Who said I cared about not being invited? What I said was I don't understand it. And yes, it's terrible about that boy. Why would someone kill a kid with cerebral palsy?"

"Why would someone kill any kid?" Missy shook her head, bewildered. "Did you really remember Olivia's birthday? Did you really know they were having a party?"

"Well, Facebook," Dora countered. "I saw a party our friends were having and didn't understand why we weren't invited. How 'bout we leave it there?"

Missy's nose wrinkled. "What's that smell?"

"What smell?"

Missy leaned toward Dora. "Are you wearing perfume or something?" she asked.

Dora shrugged, embarrassed. "I thought I'd try patchouli."

Missy tried to hide her revulsion. "Ugh!"

"Well, thank you. Like I didn't feel shitty enough, not being invited to Olivia's special-needs shindig. Now I smell too crappy for even my own girlfriend."

"Dor, we don't have a direct connection to any special-needs children. That's why we weren't invited."

Missy was taken aback by the ferocity of Dora's glare.

"We're friends. Good friends. They should have invited us. The fact that they have kids with special needs has nothing to do with this."

The doorbell chimed. The two women fell silent.

"Hello, Maverick," they heard Adam say. The rest of the conversation from the front office was too muted to follow, so Dora and Missy bided their time, boning up as they often did on investigatory techniques and sources of information—anyone and anything that might be of use to a private investigator. Much of Geller Investigations's business was catching cheating spouses or disability-insurance cheats. Adam had suggested they become students of human behavior. Was a spouse often out later than usual with a coworker or client who might be a lover? What was their behavior toward one another in public? Did they enter or exit their residences at revealing times of day? Or night?

An hour later, Adam appeared in the doorway to the back office, crutches under his arms, silently watching the two women, then continuing into the room. He sat down behind the free desk.

"We have a situation. As you know, the enthusiasm you two have shown and the results you've achieved in solving local criminal cases— specifically the four recent murders—have inspired me to do a little bit of swapping—letting you have some of the divorce and disabilities while I get back into the criminal cases." He studied his two investigators and scowled. "But my health has been too much of a distraction. I'm finding it hard to focus for more than ten or fifteen minutes at a time."

"Sorry, Adam," Missy said. Dora said nothing.

"The man who just left was Maverick Lockhart."

"So we heard," Dora confirmed. "Did you have a chance to look at his pictures? Missy sent you the links."

"I saw that they came over, but he wasn't here about his wife's cheating. His son was the young man who was killed at the Montgomery Special School two days ago."

"Oh my goodness." Dora grimaced. "How awful."

Missy's palm went to her throat.

"He's hired us to find out who killed his son. I wanted to talk to you before any of us sat down with him for a more in-depth meeting." Adam looked at them both, hope in his eyes. "We already have evidence of his wife's cheating—which is a separate thing. The books on that will be closed once he sees our photos. So, regarding his son's murder—are you up for it?"

Chapter 3

C3 leaned back on the plush crescent-shaped sectional sofa in the opulent apartment and watched Olivia, his tow-haired one-year-old daughter, play with Vanessa Burrell's sons, Drew and Buster, in the space between the two crescents. Olivia wasn't exactly playing; she was sitting, a newly acquired ability, and watching Drew, who was connecting and stacking Lego pieces into the shapes of blue and red buildings in the little alcove between the sofas. Like Olivia, Buster was sitting quietly, but unlike Olivia, he wasn't watching his brother Drew, but staring vacantly into the distance, or perhaps inward at some personal landscape.

Olivia had the flattened skull and wrinkles around the eyes that are defining features of many children with Down syndrome. She was a happy little girl who wore a blue ribbon in her hair in honor of her first birthday.

Since the murder of Julian Lockhart, C3, Sarah, and Vanessa had spoken of little else. Even when they were silent, an unspoken shared terror had sprung up among them—a terror that grew from a tiny kernel of fear they each shared as parents of special children. All three had spent much of the previous year focused on creating safe spaces for their brood.

Livvie and now Buster were children with special needs, and that demanded strength and focus from their parents. Parenting special children isn't a sprint but a marathon. The horrifying murder of Julian Lockhart at the Montgomery Special School had lit a match to the bone-deep insecurity that lived in the hearts of so many parents of special children—the fear that they couldn't possibly protect such beloved special people forever. Someday, somehow, their protection might not be enough. Someday their special child would be at the mercy of society— of the system.

C3 had stepped away from the adults to the sofa to sit with the children and quietly pray. The murder at the Montgomery School two days before had deeply shaken him. He thought of Livvie and all special young people as pristine, untouchable—perhaps because they lacked the greed and hatred that dominated so much of the media and the world.

He prayed because that's what one did with one year of clean time, or sobriety, as those in AA called it. He was more of a Narcotics Anonymous guy, since cocaine had been his true love—until he'd set eyes on his daughter.

Now that he was clean again after a devastating year-long relapse, and now that he'd finally regained his drug counseling job, he was going to follow his program to the letter. Earlier in the day he'd called LaChance, his sponsor, but LaChance hadn't yet answered. LaChance worked on Wall Street and was a successful businessman. C3 had left a short message. As soon as he'd ended the call, his phone had rung; it was Mark, one of the two men he sponsored.

"Mark," C3 said.

"Man, she did it again."

"Who?"

"Who? My wife. I asked her to buy cream cheese at the market. I need my damn cream cheese! She knows I love cream cheese. But she didn't buy it, and she didn't because she knew that would piss me off."

"You're saying she forgot to buy cream cheese at the market—*at* you?"

"Forgot? She didn't forget. She bought the kids their Chocolate Puffs cereal and their Twizzers. She didn't forget. C'mon!"

C3 sighed. "Now listen to me. Doesn't Anita do everything around your house—the cooking, the cleaning, the shopping, the washing and drying clothes …"

"Well, yeah. What's your point?"

"My point, Mark? Maybe you could forgive her. Maybe you could even buy the damn cream cheese yourself. Maybe you could help out a little more around the house."

Mark didn't answer right away, and C3 was wondering which way this would go. Would Mark curse, hang up, and maybe go out and use—buy a gram of coke?

"Hmm. I see what you're saying. She really is pretty good. Maybe even a blessing. I guess I should be grateful."

"Ya think?"

After the call, C3 felt better. There was nothing like helping a fellow addict. He smiled. Receiving that call at that moment was exactly what he had needed.

He beamed at his daughter, and love glowed in his eyes; he could watch her all day—she was the most beautiful person he'd ever seen.

Vanessa, Sarah, and Christine stood together at the floor-to-ceiling windows across the room. Vanessa was speaking quietly to Sarah and the third woman at the windows, Christine Pearsall-Bernelli, who owned the apartment, along with C3's father, Charlie Bernelli Jr. Christine was also the mayor of Beach City, while Sarah was the editor of *The Beach City Chronicle,* which she currently managed from home so she could care for Livvie.

All three women were gazing out the windows at the beach and boardwalk below. "It must have been awful." Christine, who was taller than Sarah and had just turned forty, had auburn hair in a bushy pixie cut. She shivered. "God, another murder in this town. Just what we need." Her tenure as mayor had begun after a notorious local murder that had upended the city government. She took an active interest and great pride in all things Beach City—not least of which were the magnificent miles of fine-grained sandy beach and the two-mile boardwalk and vendors that stretched in either direction below the apartment. Murder, she was quick to say, was terrible for the city's prime moneymakers— tourism, busy restaurants, and beach pass sales.

"It began as such a lovely event," Vanessa said, shifting her gaze from the beach and boardwalk to her two sons, who were across the room with C3. "The music, the people—I could feel the camaraderie you were telling me about." She turned to Sarah, who nodded and grimaced in agreement.

"We'll get through this together," Sarah said.

Vanessa's eyes watered. "That beautiful young man had the voice of an angel. And then—" She looked at Christine, and her voice faltered. "Out of nowhere …" She shook her head. "I can't go back there. I'll find help for Buster someplace else."

Sarah rubbed her hand up and down Vanessa's arm. "You'll do what you have to do for your son—for both your sons."

Vanessa looked bewildered. "For my boys to see that! How will it affect them?"

Despite her years of journalism, including news coverage of three murders, Sarah had no answer for that. "All you can do," she said, with kindness in her voice, "is be the best mom you can be."

"I can't get used to Buster being on the spectrum. I mean, how did this happen? Was it something I fed him? Will he grow out of it? How will I work? How will we afford our apartment? What will happen to Buster, and how do I explain to Drew about his Butter, which is what he's been calling Buster lately? It's like Butter is the new Buster!" She clasped her hand over Sarah's, which was still on her forearm. "How do you juggle your business and your life, your child, and your husband with such grace?"

Sarah snorted a laugh. "Grace? You ought to come and stay in our house for a day—better yet, a night!"

"How do you work from home?" Vanessa continued, her voice rising, "with the bottles, the crying, the TV, and…everything?"

As she spoke, the door to the apartment swung open, and Charlie Bernelli Jr. strode in, his arms around a large white paper bag. "Help is here!" he announced. "Shrimp scampi from The Elegant Lagoon!"

The women glanced at one another.

"Charlie," Christine began, gently chiding as she took the bag from her husband and brought it to the dining room table. She went into the kitchen for glasses and plates.

Charlie went to the bar and poured himself a few fingers of single-malt scotch. "Nothing the best shrimp in town, a few drinks, and maybe some chocolate can't fix."

C3 picked up his daughter and walked into the dining room, followed by Vanessa, who'd lifted Buster into her arms and taken Drew by the hand.

"Dad," C3 scolded, shaking his head. "You weren't there."

Charlie sipped his scotch and cupped his granddaughter's face with his free hand, ignoring his son. "How's my precious girl?"

"Still shell-shocked, like the rest of us. She witnessed a murder," C3 said, and glanced at Sarah. "Any word on who did it?"

"Nothing from the police yet," Sarah replied.

Charlie began removing plastic containers of shrimp scampi, linguini, and broccoli rabe from the white bag. Christine was pouring water and ice from a crystal pitcher into glasses and setting them in front of place settings. Using a large wooden serving spoon and fork, Charlie dished portions of the meal onto plates and passed them around the table.

Vanessa lifted Drew onto a chair and strapped Buster into a large specially-made portable car seat for toddlers on the floor. Sarah lifted Livvie into a highchair.

Once the food had been dished out and the children's bottles and meals arranged, Charlie tapped his glass with a fork. "I'd say we're due for a little good news. What do you say?" He looked at his wife.

Christine glanced around the table, her eyes suddenly twinkling. "Charlie and I found out yesterday that I'm expecting!"

• • •

Beach City's two lead homicide detectives sat at desks that were pushed together so the two men were facing one another across the span of both desks. They'd been scrutinizing data surrounding the recent influx of illegal firearms in Beach City. Arrests during the past several months had yielded a net forty percent increase in firearms seizures—many of these being semiautomatics, like AR-15s, but also such a diverse variety of handguns and rifles that the police had reached out to several nearby gun shops and ranges, requesting that their owners and management keep an eye out for unusual gun models. The request created tension between the shops and ranges, whose business model was designed to serve gun owners as well as the police, who were potentially asking these businesses to spy on their customers.

Detective Gerald Mallard wore his favorite summer suit: a Brunello Cucinelli Donegal double-breasted for which he'd paid a little over $5,000. Beneath the jacket he wore a blue Stefano Ricci silk shirt. Beneath the shirt and trousers, he wore nothing at all; he reveled in the feel of expensive material against his flesh.

He hummed happily to himself, his iPhone 14 Pro Max pressed to his ear while his wife, Kay, complained to him, first about the neighbor's hedges, which hadn't been cut in at least two weeks and extended slightly over the property line in the driveway, and then about the dogs in the houses surrounding theirs, which were noisy at hours she was sure were specifically chosen to keep her awake. The dogs, Kay claimed, also barked anytime anyone who wasn't a regular on their street so much as walked by.

Mallard listened with half an ear; Kay had obviously been drinking again. She drank every day, which led to an inevitable bout of blame;

she blamed just about everyone for just about everything. She had long ago set herself up as judge and jury for most of the people she came across. But Mallard didn't mind. He knew it was her way of coping. Alcohol and blame. Without them, she would very likely, he knew, turn her wrath on him.

Across the desks sat Ganderson, sullen and silent in his Haggar travel performance suit from JCPenney—$93.10 with a special internet code. His receding hair was dyed a shade of brown that had never been anyone's true hair color. The pockmarks on his angular face stood out under the garish fluorescent station house lighting; he was glaring to his left, which was Mallard's right. Mallard turned to see what his partner was glaring at.

Several feet in that direction stood Lieutenant Catherine Trask, holding several sheets of paper—which Mallard knew were printouts of new case files both he and his partner had access to in the BCPD computer system.

Mallard caught Trask's eye, nodded, and raised his eyebrows—inviting her to hand him the papers, though Ganderson wasn't on the phone and was obviously not busy. Lieutenant Trask and Ganderson hadn't been on speaking terms since the termination of their brief, tempestuous affair a year earlier—an affair they'd taken pains to hide but which everyone in the precinct was aware of, given that their workplace was filled, after all, with detectives.

Ganderson was giving Trask his best stink eye; Trask was giving Ganderson her best cold shoulder. Mallard held out his hand, was given the paper, and nodded for the lieutenant to leave.

Mallard scanned the paper and, when he looked up, saw that his partner was beckoning with an index finger. He slid the paper across the desks and waited while Ganderson perused its contents.

Ganderson sucked air through his teeth. "Considering that hundreds of people were there when this kid was shot, we don't have a whole lot to go on."

Mallard held up a finger. "*Au contraire mon frère.*" He paused because he knew his partner hated being kept in the dark, even for a few seconds.

"Well?"

"Cause of death: severed internal carotid artery in the neck. Brain was deprived of blood, and he bled out. Manner of death: gunshot wound to throat. Homicide. And we have a slug. A through and through. Lodged in the padding that serves as a sound baffle at the back of the stage."

"Great. But no weapon."

"No weapon," Mallard agreed.

"And no video of the area outside the auditorium?"

"Right. Video is of the interior, and of the trafficked areas—entrances and exits."

"Not the parking lot."

Mallard shook his head. "We also have the deceased. A young man."

"A *handicapped* young man," Ganderson corrected.

"A *physically challenged* young man," Mallard continued, "who was extremely talented and very popular. Perhaps someone was jealous of his talent, or of the audience's appreciation of said talent. But, at a glance, everyone loved the guy."

"Politically correct bullshit," Ganderson muttered under his breath. "How they secured a scene with so many damn wheelchairs, gurneys, IV poles, and traffic … Sounds like a mess."

"It was. We have the sound of a shot coming from the direction of one of the Montgomery School's auditorium's west-facing windows, which are at ground level outside the building." Mallard lifted his chin.

Ganderson tightened his lower lip. "And out of which no one saw anything identifying. Not the sex of any individual, number of individuals, clothing, hair—nothing."

Mallard sighed. "Except possibly a brown boot and a gold buckle, and a rifle with a scope."

Ganderson tipped his head. "Could get us somewhere. The vic's only family is his grandfather?"

"School records have his father, Maverick, and his mother, Emily, listed, but not as emergency contacts. But yeah, the kid lived with the grandfather."

Ganderson clasped his chin, his forefinger tapping his lips. "What about the kid himself?"

"What about him?" Mallard held out a hand, palm upward. "Had no enemies. Most of the kids at Montgomery don't have enemies. They lack the …" His voice trailed off.

"What was going on at the moment of the shooting?"

Mallard looked at his computer screen. "The kid was singing some song from an opera, and the school's founder—Mason Montgomery, a rich old guy—was climbing the stage to give the kid a plaque and make some sort of presentation."

"Right, and it looks like the shooting took place just as he stepped onto the stage and was approaching the kid."

The two detectives looked at one another. Mallard spoke the words they were both thinking. "What if the kid wasn't the intended target?"

Chapter 4

The next day, Dora and Missy took Freedom, Dora's rottweiler-Doberman mix, and Comfort, Missy's chocolate-colored Yorkshire terrier, for a walk on the beach. As usual, they took their walk before the nine o'clock beach opening, when the lifeguards would go on duty. Dogs were prohibited on the beach, but during Christine's tenure as mayor, they were tolerated as long as their owners cleaned up after them.

Freedom bounded in and out of the surf, her jaw open, tongue lolling. Comfort nipped at the bigger dog's heels, barking when Freedom ventured too far for him to follow. Both dogs could swim, but Comfort avoided the ocean, as he was frightened of the waves, especially when they were taller than he was, which was just about all the time. He maintained his distance and barked at the waves, perhaps in a vain attempt to stop their inexorable march toward him.

Once the dogs were walked and returned home, Dora and Missy headed for Maverick Lockhart's apartment.

The morning was typical for the second week of August—the temperature in the mid-nineties by ten, without even a hint of an ocean breeze. The beaches were overflowing with beachgoers, and even on a Wednesday, the restaurants would be reservations only.

Lockhart's building overlooked the boardwalk and beach and was slightly east of Christine and Charlie's—too far for the New York City crowds who walked from the train station to the beach at the center of town. Even so, parking was impossible to find. Dora had to park the turbo five blocks north and two east—a ten-minute walk from the car to Lockhart's apartment.

Adam had called ahead and told Lockhart to expect two of his investigators between ten and ten thirty, so they were buzzed in right away.

Dora and Missy found Lockhart waiting in an open doorway halfway down the hall and to the right of the elevator. Like so many nowadays, he eschewed shaking hands.

Maverick Lockhart had a full head of wavy gray hair that was parted on the right, a high forehead, brown-rimmed glasses, and a thin mouth. His expression was a combination of avid intelligence, confidence, and disdain. He bid the investigators sit on a white chenille couch while he sat on one of two matching armchairs. His light-brown eyes focused intently on his visitors, his palms clutched the tops of his thighs.

"I suppose you'll want to know about Julian."

"Whatever you can tell us," Dora confirmed.

He looked briefly down, then up again at his guests. "Julian was our only child. When he was born, he seemed perfect." He looked around, deciding what to say next. "As you know, my wife and I are no longer together, though technically, we're still married."

"Emily," Missy said, to confirm her name.

Lockhart didn't seem to hear her. "I hired your company originally to gather evidence that she was cheating, which I'll use in court. I saw the photos, so now everyone who needs to will know." He paused, and both Dora and Missy waited for him to continue.

He took a breath. "Julian was fine for nearly two years, though he was delayed. He didn't speak or walk when we expected, but that can happen. We didn't think anything of it at first."

"Understandable," Missy agreed.

Dora was looking around while Maverick spoke. The apartment was large and expensively furnished, but sterile. And it differed from Christine and Charlie's in that it lacked personality. The white walls, breakfront, sofa, armchairs, shelves, and even the paintings and small sculptures—all fostered an impression of wealth devoid of personality.

"Do you spend much of your time here?" Dora asked.

Lockhart equivocated. "Not really. A few weeks here and there. I travel quite a bit for business."

"What business are you in?" Dora asked.

"Business*es*." He stressed the plural.

Dora waited.

One of his eyebrows raised, and his lower lip curled slightly outward. "Nothing very exciting. Businesses that run other businesses for the most part—manufacturing here and overseas, but more the latter than the former. Here I help out small businesses and restaurants." He thought some more and made a sucking sound with his tongue. "Malls, some media. Those have been challenging of late. My business is helping businesses grow; sometimes we buy and sell them—sometimes in a hurry, while the iron's hot, so to speak." He smiled, with a trace of forced embarrassment. "But we were talking about Julian."

"How old was your son?"

Lockhart's smile faded. "Twenty-five—three weeks ago."

"Is there anybody you can think of who—"

"No!" His answer was so vehement that Missy drew back.

"I'm sorry. I'm just upset. This has been utterly devastating."

"Has there been a funeral service?" Missy asked.

Lockhart shook his head. "I have to be out of town tomorrow, and Emily and I don't see eye to eye on much of anything. She's extremely emotional."

"Understandable," Missy offered again.

"But the world must go on, you know? Business doesn't just stop."

"We understand your time is valuable, Mr. Lockhart—" Missy began.

"Maverick."

"Who watched Julian while you were away on your business trips?" Dora asked.

Lockhart looked surprised. "Oh, Julian didn't live with me. I assumed you'd been filled in by Adam."

Dora shook her head. "Not about this." Missy glanced at her; they had indeed been filled in by Adam.

"He lived with his grandfather."

"Your father?" Dora asked.

Lockhart chuckled as though at some private joke. "Hardly. Jack Ashford is Emily's father. Julian lived with Jack and received government services—entitlements—and a stipend from me." He made a bitter face.

"What's your relationship with Mr. Ashford like?" Dora asked.

"Cordial. He's okay, I guess. Devoted to Julian." He paused. "Was."

Missy asked, "You approved of his care?"

Maverick Lockhart looked at Missy for a long moment, as though trying to understand the question. "Julian didn't need as much as you might think."

Dora and Missy glanced at one another. Dora asked, "Could you please tell us as much as you can about Julian's life, his schedule, his friends, and any activities or visits he's had recently?"

"And anything that jumps out at you as being different," Missy added, "on that day."

• • •

They drove in near silence toward the Montgomery School.

"You'd think the guy would be more grief-stricken," Missy said as she turned up the car's air conditioning. "Would you mind closing your window?"

Dora enjoyed the warm summer wind on her face but did as Missy asked. "Not all fathers are warm and fuzzy. At least Lockhart seems to know he didn't have it in him to be a father, much less one who could care for a son with special needs."

"Well, but he's just lost both his wife and his son. Wouldn't you think he'd be more…"

They stopped at a light, then turned just past a sign for the Montgomery School.

Several blocks in front of them, a half dozen boys were clustered in the middle of the street. Dora smiled to herself, remembering a time she had played in the street with kids on her block, and her smile turned sad when she remembered being a small child, perhaps Drew's age, and playing catch with her father. She'd loved playing catch and hadn't thought of it in years, perhaps decades.

As they drew closer to the boys, she saw one of them, a smaller boy, standing between the car and the huddle of boys, and Dora thought she saw a sweet smile on his young face as her pleasant daydream continued. Summer days and young people playing out of doors, amidst the trees and parked cars …

As she approached, the image rearranged, and she saw frantic motion between the legs of the huddle of boys, like that in a rugby scrum. Dora now saw that the young boy with the sweet smile was no such thing; he was a lookout, and the smile on his face was a derisive snarl.

The scrum of boys, who, Dora surmised, might be football players, given their imposing size and appearance, remained in the street as several cars had to drive up on the curb to make their way around them.

Dora tapped her horn, but the young men continued to focus their attention toward the center of their huddle, where violent motion was occurring. Dora hit her horn again, this time a longer blast, and the cluster parted, revealing a smaller, twisted boy on the ground between them.

Dora put the turbo in park, opened the door, got out, and walked over to the biggest and burliest of the scrum. "What happened to him?" she asked, indicating the fallen young man.

"Who?" the boy responded, with a nasty grin.

The group converged around Dora. Several of the boys carried bats, though Dora saw no mitts or baseballs.

A horn sounded from behind Dora's car, and then another.

Dora elbowed through the closing circle with her other arm protecting her face; she bent over the boy, who was still on the ground.

He looked frightened, and he shielded his face with one arm, as afraid of Dora as he'd been of his attackers, if that's what they were.

"What's your name?" she asked.

"K-K-Kenneth," he said as Dora pulled him to his feet. Beneath him lay two crutches of the sort that include a cuff that sits at the rear of the forearm. She retrieved the crutches and helped Kenneth put them back on. When he stood, he stooped forward, on his toes, with both legs bent inward.

"K-K-Kenneth," several of the boys repeated, taunting.

"Were you on your way to school, Kenneth? Or were you leaving?" Dora asked.

"C-c-coming to school," Kenneth said.

"C-c-coming," crowed one of the boys.

"G-g-going to, to school," Kenneth said.

"G-g-going!" came more taunts.

"Why don't we take you the rest of the way. Come on, we'll just get in my car—"

"Not yet." The young man Dora had spoken to first shook his head, piggy eyes glinting from deep within his fleshy, freckled face. He turned to laugh with his friends as he grasped Kenneth by the shoulder with a meaty fist and yanked him away from Dora.

"What's your name?" Dora asked.

He looked around, then turned back to Dora, his eyes burning. "Pete."

She nodded and began to turn away, but the motion was actually a chambering of her right leg, which quickly shot out in a low side kick that smashed into the side of Pete's kneecap, shattering his patella. As he let go of Kenneth and sank, screeching, to the ground, two other boys rushed Dora from opposite sides, one from ten o'clock—front left—and the other from four o'clock—rear right. Both wielded bats. Dora whipped a left front kick to the groin of the first boy but didn't linger to watch her target crumple, his forearms crossed over his devastated privates. Instead, she instantly sank back and used the motion to elbow the second boy in the gut with the full weight of her body behind the blow, catching his bat mid-swing at a point close to his fist, where its motion was weakest. The elbow elicited a whoosh of air and a pained "Whuh!" as the bat sailed away.

She stood facing the three remaining footballers, bouncing lightly on her toes, fists in front of her, elbows tight against her ribs. "Why don't you go get some replacements. But get at least five this time, and make sure everyone's wearing cups and pads. And hey, feel free to bring bats or whatever you've got. I'll be right here."

She looked down at the first boy, who was on the ground, whimpering. "Like making fun of people with special needs? Hey! I'm asking you a question, Pete."

The boy's mouth opened and closed several times. "Nuh, nuh, no."

She nodded slowly. "Now you can think about how it is to live with a physical challenge. And look, I can always make sure you have more than one challenge, okay? Maybe you need to see how it is to live like Kenneth here."

"I—I'm calling the cops, lady."

Dora laughed. "Go for it. Let the whole world know how some girl whupped all of you—two of you with bats—while you were picking on a young man with a disability. In fact, I'll call my friend, Sarah Turner—

she's the editor of *The Chronicle*. People need to hear about you and your pals, don't you think?"

When Pete didn't answer, Dora turned and helped Kenneth toward her car, where Missy was waiting, a palm shading her eyes.

Dora turned and yelled back to the group of boys. "Maybe you ought to think about some charity work for people with special needs! That's what some football teams do, you know—if that's what you are. That's what real men do—help others."

She and Missy drove Kenneth the rest of the way to the Montgomery School, where he walked slowly into the building between the two investigators.

Chapter 5

Principal Claire Sumner was a slender woman in her early sixties, with a bright smile and neatly trimmed, shoulder-length auburn hair. She was dressed in a modest sapphire dress and matching shoes with low heels. And she was all business.

"Walk with me," she said to Missy and Dora, then quickly set off down the hall, her blue heels clacking on the shiny green tiles.

"The class we'll be visiting consists of a half dozen young adults. Despite its name, Montgomery isn't really a school, but a day care wing of Montgomery Care, which offers a continuum of care, from school-type learning to care for the extremely disabled who need around-the-clock help. Some live here, and for them we're a hospital of sorts—perhaps even a nursing home. The room we're going to includes people who come here during the day, ranging from age eighteen through their late thirties, and the ratio of caregivers is two to one."

"Is that good?" Missy asked.

"Typically you'll find about six to one. I've chosen this class because these folks are less emotionally fragile. I'd like for you to first observe them through a doorway viewer, and then we'll speak with them one-on-one, with myself and a caregiver overseeing to steer clear of any trauma. We don't want to focus on the actual shooting, but on anything they saw that could help with your investigation. That might be tricky, so I'll facilitate."

The door to the group room was solid wood with a steel-reinforced clear plastic see-through rectangle at eye level. Sumner opened the door to the room, leaned in, and spoke a few words, then returned to Dora and

Missy, followed by a young Black man with close-cropped hair, a mustache and beard, sad eyes, and creases in his forehead that gave him a concerned, caring look.

"This is Robert, the lead caregiver for this group. Robert will explain to you who's who and help us navigate the questions and answers."

Robert smiled at Dora and Missy, then turned his attention to the door's viewing window.

Music was playing inside the room, and a lanky man was waving his hands in the air. The others in the room followed suit to varying degrees. The man was clean-shaven, in his thirties, of medium height, with sharp brown eyes, a thin nose, and wavy brown hair parted on the left side.

"That's Sean," Robert said. Sean was smiling, and most of the rest of the group smiled too. He waved his hands high over his head, then low and close to the ground. Many of the others in the room did the same. Several were laughing, taking their cue from Sean.

"That's Leslie." Robert indicated a young woman in a pink dress with straight, straw-colored hair that fell to just over her ears. Dora could see that she had Down syndrome.

"William prefers to watch," Robert said, pointing to a massive young blond man in blue overalls and a white T-shirt who was standing off to one side. William's eyes met Dora's, then wandered away. He seemed not to focus on any one thing—instead looking at his group mates, at objects in the room, or at his own fingers.

"Lenny likes to dress warm up top, even though it's summer." Lenny was a short, thick young man with Down syndrome. He had heavy black eyebrows and a mustache, and wore a brown coat over a yellow T-shirt and beige shorts, along with black high-top sneakers. "Lenny always wears shorts, even in the winter." Robert's face brightened, and he stepped back. "And that's our Penny—we call her Penny Bright."

A full-figured woman in a red-and-blue checkered dress was smiling and pointing to each person in the room; her voice rose cheerfully above the music.

"Hi, Leslie! Hi, Sean! Hi, William!" She danced happily around the room, her hair whirling a small circle as she laughed to herself. She didn't follow the others' movements, but twirled from one end of the room to the other, touching the walls and door, and pressing her enormous brown eyes to the clear plastic rectangle in the door. "Hi, Robert! Hi, Lady One! Hi, Lady Two!" She grinned and danced away again.

"If you ever need cheering up," Robert said, tipping his head toward Penny, "Penny Bright's your girl."

As they watched, a handsome ebony man with prominent cheekbones and watchful eyes helped Kenneth into the room. Dora and Missy glanced at one another, remembering him from the violent encounter with the football players. He seemed none the worse for wear.

"Hi, Kelvin!" Penny cried. "Hi Sharleece!" She waved to a woman in her mid-twenties with thick, curly black hair that fell to just below her shoulders. Her wide, bright smile rounded her deep-brown cheeks and formed dimples at either side of her mouth. Sharleece, in a sleeveless black-and-white striped dress, followed the movements of the group through her rectangular gray-framed glasses.

"Sharleece, Kelvin, Sean, and I are with this group every day," Robert explained. "Continuity is important for our people."

"Who's that?" Missy nodded toward a figure that was pressed against the corner at the opposite side of the room.

"That's Marshall. He's a dual diagnosis. I don't think we'll be inter-viewing Marshall." Robert looked serious, then brightened. "But every-one else is a go."

• • •

The answers the special young people gave to Dora and Missy's questions, which were approved by Principal Sumner and relayed by Robert, varied in relevance. When reminded about the performance at the assembly and asked what they'd seen, Leslie said, "I saw a piano!"

Penny said, "I saw Robert, and Sean, and Kelvin, and Mrs. Sumner, and Julian—" Upon mentioning Julian, she stopped her exuberant nam-ing of those in attendance. Her face fell, and she looked into her lap, re-fusing to speak further.

"Did anyone notice anything outside the window?" Robert asked. Missy had provided the question.

"I saw a shoe," Kenneth said. "And a broom handle."

"I saw a lady," William said. "She had long brown hair and a beard."

"The woman had a beard?" Robert asked.

"I saw a man." William corrected himself. "A man with long hair."

"What else did you see?" Dora asked.

"I saw a man," William said again.

"Did the man do anything?" Robert asked.

"He was looking, with a stick," William added. Then he said, "I heard a truck."

"I heard a firecracker," Penny said, and her face again grew animat-ed.

"I saw a stick! I saw a man! I saw a beard!" Penny crowed.

"People were crying," Kenneth said.

Penny began to cry. Within seconds, all of the special people were crying.

"I have to pee," Kenneth said.

Robert gave Dora and Missy a look that said they were done.

• • •

The buzzer inside the vestibule sounded. Kelvin opened the door and made his way to the elevator. He wasn't sure what to expect, as the social worker at the Montgomery School had only directed him to a family who needed help with a very young child with special needs. When he'd seen the address and the family name, he'd understood and volunteered immediately.

Since his wife's death, Kelvin had curtailed his music career and focused on training to be an aide or companion to people with special needs. He'd stayed away from music entirely for nearly a year but had recently begun playing piano again, which he found to be a balm. It was as if his fingers thanked him after he played. So he tried singing and found that this, too, brought comfort. He loved music, and music loved him, and perhaps he would again find his way back to playing for people, entertaining, communing—reveling in his music.

He rang the bell on the apartment door, which was answered by the same attractive young woman with long dreads and a warm smile he'd known several years earlier.

Vanessa gasped. "Kelvin!" She threw her arms around him and pulled him to her.

"Hey, Nessa. When I saw it was you, I had to come."

She stood aside for him to enter the apartment. That's when he heard the screams.

He tried not to cringe, though the screams were so loud and piercing that he found it difficult not to react. "Is that …"

"Buster. We're just figuring out that he's apparently on the spectrum."

Vanessa stood with Kelvin at the entrance to the living room. The screams came from a doorway in the hall behind them. Kelvin could see the stress in the lines around Vanessa's eyes and mouth, which she pressed closed when she finished speaking. Now that he saw her more closely, he could see that she seemed to have aged.

As Vanessa left the room, Kelvin sat down on the couch and bent to look at the pictures on the table to his right. In the largest of these, Vanessa's husband had his arm around her; their older son was smiling between them. All three grasped a bassinet that held a baby who must have been Buster several years earlier. Surrounding the family image were smaller, silver-framed individual photos of each family member— each with a bright smile.

Vanessa appeared in the doorway to the hall that led to the bedrooms. She was holding Buster to her chest. His screams had faded to muffled sobs now that he was with his mother.

"Hey there, Buster," Kelvin said, his voice soft and sweet. "Remember me? You helped me when I was feeling bad a while back."

Buster looked at Kelvin. Slowly, his sobs subsided.

"How—how did you do that?" Vanessa was astonished. "He's never stopped crying with anyone besides his brother or me before—and even then, it takes a while. That's—wow!"

"I love children," Kelvin purred. "Simple as that, and I think he remembers me. After Martine passed, Buster helped me by getting me to sing with him. Love remembers. I'm returning the favor." He held out his hands for Vanessa to hand Buster to him.

"He won't let anyone but me—" Vanessa warned.

But Kelvin had already lifted Buster from Vanessa and set him on his thigh. Buster hiccuped but was otherwise silent.

Vanessa gave a sharp inhale. "His eyes."

Buster was looking at Kelvin's face with avid interest.

"Thank you, Lord!" Vanessa breathed.

Kelvin ducked his head and looked Buster in the eyes, and Buster looked back at him.

Vanessa said, "He never looks right at anyone."

"Shhh," Kelvin said softly. Then he sang, "You'll sing a song. I'll sing a song. We'll sing a song together …"

Buster's eyes grew wide. He smiled.

"Oh my goodness!" Vanessa mouthed, her palms to either side of her mouth. "A miracle!"

Kelvin sang five songs, and Buster continued to watch and listen, smiling intermittently, and at times looking away.

Finally, he drifted off to sleep, so Kelvin carried him to his bedroom, where Drew was playing with a miniature train set. Vanessa followed and put a finger to her lips to let Drew know his brother was going to sleep.

Kelvin gently laid the sleeping Buster down on his bed and covered him with his blanket. When Kelvin stood up again, he found himself in a long, tight hug.

Chapter 6

The next afternoon, Vanessa spent nearly an hour venting on the phone with Sarah, who told Lemieux, Esther, and the team at *The Chronicle* that she was "in a meeting." Sarah understood as none of her friends and family did the challenges of having a special child. As it happened, both women needed to vent and share their respective traumas, and who better than each other? They shared the trauma of having witnessed the murder of a gifted young music lover who happened to have special needs while being themselves parents of children with special needs. They shared their focus on keeping their children safe in an unsafe world, and they vowed to support one another, hold one another's hand, and protect one another's children—whatever may come.

Later, Vanessa walked quietly around the blue-lit production area on the second floor of her job at The Bernelli Group's offices. The area featured six desks, and on each was a MacBook Pro. There was a glass-separated area for proofreaders and two doors leading to and from the production area—one to an office, the other to an elevator and the stairs.

She'd hired Kelvin on the spot to babysit her boys, then reached out to Nia Paulson, who had been scheduled to sit, to cancel. Luckily Nia was understanding about the situation and was okay with the last-minute cancellation.

The desk and computer one encountered upon entering the room were designated as Vanessa's. She was rarely involved in designing—though Luis, Bernelli's chief designer, had been teaching her. She was the evening manager, a nebulous title that gave her the responsibility for just about everything that occurred on the second shift—including reviewing incoming materials, handing the work out to the designers (which today was only Luis), checking the proofreaders' work, and overseeing operations to make sure the shift ran smoothly.

She stood behind Luis as he worked on imagery of rippling chocolate in Photoshop. He was shifting his head first to one side and then the other, looking at his screen from different angles. His light-brown skin turned turquoise in the reflected light from his screen.

"One second there was music," she was saying, "then not even a bang; it was more of a cracking sound. Next thing I knew, the whole place went crazy. When the cops came, we were all on the floor, then they herded us down a hallway to the cafeteria."

Luis continued working and spoke without turning around. "How are your kids doing?"

Vanessa considered the question. "Drew has been asking if a man is going to shoot him through the bedroom window." She sighed. "If Buster is really on the spectrum, I'll have to figure out where to send him, if anywhere. I thought Montgomery had the best reputation. But now?"

Luis turned, concern in his eyes. "Who's with them now?"

"A musician I used to know who happens to work at Montgomery as an aide. Buster was doing his screaming thing again, and somehow Kelvin calmed him right down, then sang to him, and Buster was quiet and paid attention. You could have knocked me over with a feather."

"Wow," Luis said, and turned back to his screen.

"Know what's crazy? Couple of years ago, Kelvin lost his wife. He fell apart, and music is what healed him."

"I believe that," Luis said.

"But the crazy part is Buster helped him. Buster sang to Kelvin, and Kelvin responded when nothing else worked. Buster's singing is what started him on the road to healing."

Luis turned and locked eyes with Vanessa. "Whoa!"

Charlie Bernelli kept only the one designer, Luis, on staff, since the ebb and flow of work didn't justify more. He brought in freelancers—who were private contractors—and let them go as the workflow warranted. Today the team was working on graphics for a candy bar wrapper, a supporting sell sheet, and a shipping box for a new client, Benjamin Schucker, and his new product, Benny's Bar.

Initially, Vanessa, Luis, Michele the office manager, and Brian a proofreader, had been excited to work on this particular job. For three whole shifts, they'd worked with a portable cooking pot, melting and pouring chocolate, and photographing the results to use for illustration purposes. The fun had ended abruptly when Benny himself had come in to oversee production. Charlie had proudly walked the new client around the floor, pointing out the work that was being done, and exuberantly co-daydreamed about the creative process and the coming design evolutions.

Schucker immediately found fault with the work. Why had this font been chosen? Why was this shade of brown being used and not that one? You call that chocolate? What kind of slogan was "Benny's Better Bar. It's Benelicious"?

The Bernelli Group's employees were all professionals who were accustomed to clients' suggestions and ideas, even criticisms. What they weren't used to was screaming. Benny ramped up his criticisms until he was yelling disdainfully, as though to a five-year-old, and Charlie made matters worse by coddling Schucker, agreeing with everything he said and promising to ride herd on his production staff, who, he agreed, were obviously falling short of their potential.

But what could the staff do? This was life in the advertising industry. They continued working, doing their best to usher creative concepts past the scraggly, sallow-skinned client with his body odor and bad teeth.

"That's pretty good, Luis," Vanessa said, and Luis smiled gratefully. "We need to give him a few alts. Add a little red to your brown in one, a little yellow in another, then dupe all three and change the headline font to Poster Bodoni."

Luis nodded and refocused his attention toward his computer screens.

Vanessa couldn't help but overhear Charlie, who was on the phone in his office.

"Are you just nauseous or are you throwing up?" A pause. "Well, sweetheart, stay home then. It's your body, and you're the boss! Aw, who cares what they think? The city will run fine without you for a day. Yes, I know you haven't missed a day in— So work, but work from home, and for God's sake, near a bathroom." Charlie was silent for a long moment. "I feel the same way, Chris. Murder isn't good for tourism or the restaurant business. I mean, who is it good for besides maybe the murderer? And even then. But honey, we've been down this road before. If I try to tell Sarah how to run her newspaper and downplay certain stories, I know her. She'll do the opposite. She'll add in editorials or sidebars. Honey, honey, I'm on your side. I am! I have skin in the game. I have clients who need smooth sailing in Beach City, and I have you!"

Vanessa heard Charlie exhale a long sigh. "I know. We have a good police force," he said. "Terry Stalwell's a good man who runs a tight ship, and the Goose and the Gander are good homicide detectives. It's nobody's fault we've had a bad few years, except maybe the murderers'. I understand Terry has a car watching the Montgomery School now all day every day."

• • •

But Sarah Turner wasn't focused on *The Chronicle*'s stories surrounding the murder at the Montgomery Special School. She'd run stories she and Lemieux had written based on her own experience at the event and additional spotty information supplied by her stringers—unpaid journalism students and wannabes. She'd run fact-focused stories about what had occurred, about the school's official reaction—which was nothing, which was itself a story. She considered a story about the police chief's reaction—there was none, which wasn't a story she could run, as long as she desired a working relationship with the BCPD, which she certainly did. She attempted to get an interview with Julian Lockhart's guardian—his grandfather, Jack Ashford. But her stringer had been chased off the property by—she found this hard to believe—an old man with a rifle. She was also considering interviewing the families of other attendees of the Montgomery School.

But, at the moment, Sarah wasn't focused on any of this. Nor was she focused on her daughter, Livvie, who, thank goodness, was sleeping. Sarah was focused on keeping *The Chronicle* afloat. She could handle juggling her stringers; her two extremely overworked office jacks-of-all-trades, Lemieux and Esther; the dissemination of news; the perpetual public outcry; the incessant and often inane feedback from the city (aka her de facto mother-in-law, Christine Pearsall); the unions; the businesses; and the often bizarre intermingling of all of these.

What she couldn't cope with—what was utterly beyond her—were the news website's financial woes. She'd inherited a team of contractor salespeople from her predecessor, the now-jailed Tom Volkov. But ever since COVID struck in early 2020, the advertising had first slowed to a trickle and finally all but dried up. It was a blessing that Charlie Bernelli continued to run his ongoing self-funded tourism campaign, which somehow made a little money, and Christine had generously committed to running ads supporting city events that Sarah would have had to report on anyway, as the events were in the public interest.

She sat at her laptop, glancing at her gorgeous, love-of-her-life daughter, who was sleeping peacefully, and choked back tears as realization dawned and she felt impelled to write the editorial that would appear in the following week's edition—an editorial announcing the closing of *The Chronicle* due to insufficient funds and impending bankruptcy. After writing the editorial, she put it aside. She wouldn't publish it—yet.

A half-hour later, she heard the key in the door to the apartment, and there was C3, cradling her head to his chest and telling her it was going to be okay—which she knew was kind, misinformed, and far, far from the truth.

Chapter 7

"I know this is difficult, Mr. Ashford, is it?" Mallard looked the man in the doorway directly in the eye while Ganderson examined his demeanor and clothing from a foot behind his partner.

"That's right. Jack Ashford." The man ran a hand back over his long gray hair. His narrow eyes were surrounded by wrinkles. They were wrinkles born of amusement and laughter—even joy. But no one was laughing now, and nobody shook hands.

Jack Ashford's house was an amber three-story Victorian with deep-red pillars. It overlooked the bay on the north side of town. The detectives introduced themselves and showed badges, then Ashford invited them in.

They passed through a living room that was filled with photos of Julian—on end tables, on the mantle, on shelves. Julian with his grandfather, Julian with friends, Julian singing with a choir and singing solo in a spotlight on a stage. There was also a photo of a youthful blonde woman who looked like Jack and who Mallard assumed must be Emily—Julian's mother and Jack's daughter. There were no photos of Julian with either of his parents.

Ashford led them into a dining room and sat down at the table; the two detectives sat opposite.

Mallard cleared his throat. "We're sorry to put you through this, Mr. Ashford. We know it's a difficult time."

"I'll tell you what's difficult," Ashford said, "newspaper people calling and banging on my door all hours. Don't suppose you can do anything about them?"

"They're just doing their job. It's unpleasant, but it's their job," Ganderson explained.

Mallard spoke while Ganderson rose and squinted at the photos. "How did your grandson get to and from Montgomery?"

"They provided a van with a lift, but occasionally he asked to be let off a few blocks away so he could walk a bit and enjoy the sunshine. He and a friend, Kenneth, sometimes did this together."

Mallard noted that Ashford was gaunt and wan, despite the laugh lines around his eyes.

"Besides this Kenneth, who interacted with him from the time he left the house until he returned home?" Ganderson asked.

Ashford took a deep breath, sat back, and folded his arms across his chest. "Well, there'd be the bus driver, and aides they have outside the building and in the hallways to facilitate everyone getting where they need to go. They have caregivers and special-needs teachers, and Julian had PT, OT, and speech therapy weekly. Let's see—medical personnel, of course." He blinked, thinking. "And there'd be administrators around, here and there. Ms. Sumner and the office staff, but I couldn't tell you much about them."

"Er, ah, were you there often?" Mallard queried. "Would you recognize these people?"

"Too many. I was there early on, to help Julian." He paused, choking on his grandson's name. "To help him get settled. Maybe I'd recognize a few. There was turnover among the caregivers and aides, who were contractors, I believe. The nurses, therapists, and medical personnel were on staff. They tended to be more permanent, but, you know." He shrugged helplessly and held out his hands, palms up. He blinked again, suddenly upset. "You think one of them might have—"

"We're trying to get as clear a picture as possible before drawing any conclusions," Mallard explained as he picked a piece of lint from his freshly pressed lapel.

"Did you receive training to help you to care for Julian?" Ganderson asked. He sat down and leaned forward, his elbows on his knees.

"I did, at first. I can handle everything now," he answered proudly, then caught himself. "I could … I did, that is."

Ganderson drew a breath and was about to speak, but Ashford was looking at the backs of his hands and shaking his head. "I'm on Social Security and a small teacher's pension. My wife, God rest her, was the one with the serious paycheck. She supervised a team of programmers in the city. But me? What else was I going to do but care for my grandson? It was a no-brainer."

He ran his hand back through his hair again. "You know, sometimes it was like he wasn't even a separate person but a working part of my mind. My conscience, in a way." He laughed bitterly. "Pretty selfish. I'd been a music teacher, and I used to play piano for Julian when he was little. He had difficulty speaking. The muscles involved were affected by his CP. But you know what? When he sang, all that was gone."

Ashford smiled, and the weight that had been on his shoulders seemed to melt away. "We'd joked about him singing all the time, instead of speaking, I mean. He could sing to the bus driver, to the other folks on the bus or at Montgomery, to the clerk at the store." He chuckled. "He could sing the phone book." Then his eyes cleared and the weight returned. His shoulders sagged.

Mallard glanced at Ganderson, who nodded. "What else can you tell us about your grandson?" Mallard encouraged.

Ashford started to speak, clearing his throat several times. "Have either of you actually heard him sing?" he asked.

Both detectives shook their heads. "Haven't had the pleasure," Ganderson replied.

"And a pleasure it would have been if you had," Ashford promised. "The boy— Well, he wasn't a boy anymore, was he? He could sing like an angel. In fact, he was an angel, as far as I'm concerned." He paused. "He is now, anyway."

"Who else did he come in contact with?" Ganderson asked. "Why would anybody—"

"That's right!" Ashford blurted, leaning forward. "Why would anybody want to hurt him, to kill him?" He was suddenly breathing heavily.

"What about you, Mr. Ashford," Ganderson asked.

"Me?" Ashford drew back, his eyes blazing. "You think I would—"

"No," Mallard gently replied. "What my partner meant was, we understand that Julian had no enemies, but do you? Do you have any enemies? Anyone who might want to hurt you through Julian?"

Ashford stilled, his palms on his knees; his eyes wandered around the room. Slowly, he shook his head. "I'm just a retired music teacher."

"What about ex-students?" Mallard continued. "High school kids can get pretty fired up about misunderstandings. You taught high school?"

Ashford continued shaking his head. "Well, that was all so long ago."

"Think about it," Ganderson advised.

Ashford began to cough. His eyes watered.

"Are you okay, Mr. Ashford?" Mallard asked. "Can I get you some water?"

Ashford swallowed several times and took a moment to get his breath. "I'm fine. Don't you worry about me."

"You were about to tell us more about your grandson," Mallard reminded him.

Ashford nodded and smiled sheepishly. "I'm sorry. People say I was looking after the boy, but we were looking after each other. Without him, I don't know what I'll— But here I am again, not telling you about him. And that's what you asked, isn't it?"

The detectives waited.

"We loved to fish. I had to set the line up for him, but once set up, he had a knack for knowing where the fish were. He could think like a fish, he used to say." The old man chuckled to himself, and Mallard could see Jack Ashford's face as it was meant to be—the sunny smile of a joyful grandfather. "But we had to give it up."

"Why's that?" Ganderson asked.

Ashford shook his head. "Boy was too compassionate. He felt bad for the fish." He shrugged. "But that was Julian. Singing was his real love. And checkers."

"Checkers?" Mallard repeated.

Ashford nodded. "Beat me often too. We played checkers and listened to classical music every Sunday afternoon when it wasn't football season."

"Who'd he root for?" Mallard asked.

"Giants. Loved the old linebackers—the ones before his time, like L. T., Banks, Van Pelt—even Sam Huff. He'd find videos on YouTube."

"No kidding?" Mallard was impressed.

"No kidding. He accepted that he couldn't run and play most sports, but he was happy for those who could."

Ganderson was glancing around again at the photos. "Your daughter?" He indicated a picture of a blonde woman with narrow blue eyes, but hers lacked laugh lines.

Ashford nodded. "That's my Emily."

"Why wasn't Julian with his mother?" Ganderson continued.

Ashford's face went pensive; his mouth twisted with regret, and he looked down as he spoke. "Emily was told she was having a baby that was at a high risk for some abnormality—though cerebral palsy can't be detected before birth. She was beside herself about that. She felt she couldn't care for a child with special needs, and yet she couldn't bear to have an abortion. She was caught between a rock and a hard place. She felt he was a human being who deserved a chance at life, yet once born, she couldn't be the one to give it to him." He looked up at the detectives. "My daughter's choices were both heartbreaking and none of my business. It's not my place to judge. What was my place was to offer any help I could. So I raised Julian."

"Did he ever visit his mother?" Ganderson asked.

Ashford shook his head. "She wanted it in writing that she'd never see him. She didn't trust herself and was afraid they'd bond—that he'd be drawn to her. She didn't want to put that on his shoulders; she felt she'd done enough damage by giving him up. She was hard on herself."

Ganderson snorted. "Maybe she was hard on him."

Ashford gave the detective a long look. "I love my daughter, Detective, and I love—loved—Julian. While I'm on God's green earth, I'd do just about anything for either of them."

"Er, ah, what about the father?" Mallard asked.

"What about Maverick Lockhart?" Ganderson emphasized.

"What about him?" Ashford responded impassively.

Ganderson asked, "What can you tell me about him?"

"Nothing."

"Nothing?"

"Not a thing. You want to know about him, you go find him." The kind old man had vanished, replaced by cold steel.

"One other thing," Ganderson said. "What's your opinion of the Montgomery School?"

"No comment."

"No comment?"

"That's what I said. He went there in the morning. Came back at night—except the last day. While he was there, they did some things. That's about it. But let me ask you guys something. Do either of you have grandkids?"

Both detectives shook their heads.

"Well then, you don't know what love is. I never loved anything like I loved that boy."

As the detectives left, tears were streaming down Jack Ashford's cheeks.

Chapter 8

Dora and Missy drove along the avenue that ran just north of the beach. The street was filled with beachgoers in bathing suits carrying beach chairs and wheeling carts filled with children, toys, umbrellas, and coolers. All were heading to the beach. Cars drove slowly along every street, their drivers searching for that white whale of summertime in Beach City: a parking spot.

"It doesn't matter that we aren't part of the special-needs community. We've been friends with C3 and Sarah, not to mention Charlie and Christine, since long before Olivia was born. Who else did they invite? Other parents of special kids? Okay. But we supposedly care for one another, so invite us too."

Dora's voice rose as she spoke, and her tone increased in vehemence. "We knew them before they knew any of those folks."

Missy knew Dora's temper and how hurt feelings over seemingly insignificant slights could send her lover into agonized rages that could take hours, sometimes days, to dissipate. "Maybe they'll have another get-together and invite us."

"When?" Dora turned a corner without slowing down.

Missy drew a quick breath and gripped Dora's thigh. "Well," she began.

"Yeah, well. Olivia's birthday's passed, and we haven't heard a thing out of them, so you know what? Pfft!" Dora made a flicking motion with the tips of the fingers of one hand, as though flicking away a fly.

"Just remember," Missy said in her sweetest, most placating tone. "I love you."

The anger and hurt vanished from Dora's face and were replaced by a sunny smile. "Oh yeah. Right. I kind of forgot. I love you too, Miss." She turned her head and met Missy's inclined face, kissing her lightly on the lips as they pulled up in front of a rather dilapidated apartment house on a three-block stretch of road that housed some of the least expensive, most run-down abodes. The last block of the run-down apartments was only a block from the Montgomery School, so this apartment building was literally a stone's throw from the special-needs facility.

Once the car was parked, Missy got out and hung back as Dora crossed the street and started up the broken sidewalk toward the front door.

"Come on, Miss," Dora beckoned. "I need you to wear your librarian hat. Focus!" Missy's part-time work as a reference librarian had come in handy on more than one occasion.

Missy scanned the list of residents next to the column of door buzzers. Many were simply names scrawled on pieces of paper that had been taped to the scuffed metal surface.

"D. Moran" was next to 4D. Missy pressed the buzzer. A few moments later, another buzzer replied, and they entered the tenement and started up the four flights of stairs, avoiding the many broken tiles along the way.

When they arrived on the fourth floor, Missy took a moment to rest before they walked first one way and then the other in search of 4D. They found the door and knocked, as there was no buzzer or bell.

The door opened the several inches that the heavy chain allowed, and a pair of black eyes sunk deep into a bony face looked out at them. "Well?"

"Ms. Moran?" Missy began.

"Who's askin'?"

"We're looking into the murder that took place several days ago at the Montgomery School."

The door was opened by a rail-thin woman in tight, dirty black jeans tucked into brown leather boots and a loose-fitting forest-green boat-neck shirt. The woman glanced at Dora and Missy, turned, and walked farther into the apartment.

Dora followed, and Missy followed Dora.

The apartment was in the railroad style—a chain of rooms along a hallway. The front door led to a living room, which led to a kitchen, which led to a bedroom. The woman walked through a short hallway, turned, and continued through a wide arched doorway into a living room that was painted brown. Nothing hung on the brown walls, whose color loosely matched the thick shag carpet. A lit unfiltered cigarette burned in an amber glass ashtray. The woman sat down, tapped the ashes from the cigarette, took a drag, and exhaled smoke toward her guests.

Dora asked, "You're Diana Moran?"

The woman didn't answer.

Missy wrinkled her nose at the smoke. "We're here about the—"

"You already told me that."

The woman's face had a gaunt, cadaverous look; a network of veins showed on her temples.

"Do you have any idea why anyone would want to kill that young man?" Dora asked.

"Let me tell you about the Montgomery School." The woman nod-ded in the direction of the hallway from which they'd come. From farther along that hallway came the sound of a TV. "I've lived here for thirty-three years—long before that place showed up." She pointed a bony finger. "I didn't ask them to come. I didn't want people like that on my street. I went to city hall when they had their meetings."

"Meetings?" Missy asked.

"Permitting meetings—supposedly to see what public opinion was. Well, I'm the public, and I gave my opinion. I didn't want them here. They should be in a special place—a place just for people like that."

Dora frowned. "People like what?"

Moran gave Dora a hard look. "You know what people. People who can't walk or talk or think right. And they call them special? Who're they kidding! Nothing special about them. They're the opposite." Moran spat the words at them, and Missy recoiled.

Dora drew a deep breath, let it out, and took another, which she held for a few seconds and let out more slowly. "I understand you were at the event where the boy was killed."

Moran didn't answer.

"Why?" Dora asked. "You hate the place so much. Why would you go to an event where you'd have to listen to these people you can't stand —people who are so obviously inferior to you?"

Diana Moran looked at Dora more closely, as though trying to decide whether Dora had meant what she said and was complimenting her or was being sarcastic and insulting her.

"I go to keep an eye on them." Moran's eyes looked from Dora to Missy and back again. "I go because I want to know what they're planning next. Maybe they're planning on expanding. Who knows?" She shrugged a bony shoulder.

Missy nodded. "Did you see what happened?"

The corners of Moran's mouth tightened, but she didn't answer.

"Did you see who shot him?" Dora asked.

Moran stared back at her. Finally, she shook her head.

Dora pressed her. "Nothing?"

She shook her head again.

"What about when you left the building?" Dora asked.

Moran's lips tightened; she shook her head a third time.

Dora jutted her face toward Moran. "You glad the boy's dead?"

Missy clasped Dora's forearm. "Dor. Let's go."

Moran smiled; it was an ugly smile, but it looked at home on her face. "I don't care one way or another. I just want to be able to live in peace without God-knows-what moving in all around me. I want to watch my *Law & Order.* You might not like me, but I know what's legal and illegal. I've learned a thing or two about the law from that show. I know all about police science. That show's made me an expert." She smiled again, this time with something that on another face might have passed for pride.

Dora stood and left space for Missy to stand and walk toward the hall and the front door.

"Well, wasn't that nice," Dora said, as they left the tenement and emerged into the sunlight.

• • •

When Dora and Missy returned to the Geller Investigations office, a furniture van was pulling away, and when they stepped into the back room that served as Adam Geller's permanent office and Dora and Missy's temporary one, they stopped in the doorway and stared. Two brand-new wooden desks and upholstered office chairs filled the right side of the room, opposite Adam's desk on the left. On each desk sat an unboxed computer. Adam was nowhere to be seen.

Missy grinned at Dora, who raised an eyebrow.

"Looks like you girls might be staying awhile," Thelma brayed from behind her desk in the front room. They heard her chair slide back, and she appeared in the doorway, grinning. "You can do your one-tough-bitch routine," she said, pointing her chin at Dora, "and you can be the know-it-all librarian," she chinned at Missy, "from your very own official base stations."

"Gee, thanks," Missy said.

"Where's the boss?" Dora asked.

"MSK," Thelma replied, meaning Memorial Sloan Kettering, the cancer hospital in New York City. "Radiation all week. He'll probably be in later if he's up to it."

The two investigators tested out their new chairs, swiveling back and forth. Missy had headed for the rear desk, leaving the front for Dora, whom she saw as the senior partner. She got up, went to the computer on Dora's desk, and opened the top of the box. "Mind if I set these up?"

"Be my guest," Dora replied. "But we ought to get going. Our appointment with Gloria Steinmetz, Penelope's mother, is at two, and Frederick Chase is at three thirty."

"Easy peasy," Missy said and got to work.

Once the computers were set up and connected to the office Wi-Fi, Dora and Missy headed out into what was turning into one of the hottest days in memory—well into triple digits.

Gloria Steinmetz and her husband, Jason, lived on a tree-lined street several blocks from the beach in the center of town. The oak and maple trees were many decades old, and their tops had grown together, shading the street beneath a canopy of leaves, leaving the street, sidewalk, and front lawns and gardens of the homes below them sprinkled with bright bits of sunlight.

Dora and Missy walked up the brick steps of the gray stone colonial home and rang the bell. The door was quickly answered by a diminutive woman with pale, pimply skin and short red hair that was complemented by red-rimmed glasses.

"You're the investigators?" she asked.

"Dora Ellison and Missy Winters." Dora indicated Missy with one hand.

"Gloria Steinmetz." The woman held the door and ushered Dora and Missy past a white staircase and into a white living room with shiny Naugahyde couches, a painted white wooden coffee table covered with picture books of Europe, and two end tables, also laden with travel books.

"Can I get you something?"

"No, thanks," Dora and Missy said simultaneously. They had sat down next to one another on the couch, which squeaked when they sat.

"Are you sure? I'm having tea. It's no trouble." She disappeared into a hallway and could be heard filling a kettle.

"That's okay, thanks," Dora said.

Mrs. Steinmetz continued talking from the kitchen, but Dora heard only fragments of what she was saying. She heard, "Penelope seems to be … of course that's … but they do a good job with … safety first!"

She returned with her tea, seeming not to notice her guests' lack of feedback, and settled into one of the armchairs. "So, do you have specific questions?"

"Your daughter is Penny?" Missy began.

"Penelope, but people do call her Penny." Mrs. Steinmetz nodded and sipped her tea in small audible slurps. "Penny Bright," she added. "Because she's so cheerful!"

"How has she coped with the murder at Montgomery?" Dora asked.

Mrs. Steinmetz pursed her lips. "She was utterly devastated for two days. Then there was the weekend, and, as Penelope does, she distracted herself with her videos. She loves musical shows, and we have lots of them. YouTube has lots more, of course. She puts them on, and for her, everything else vanishes. She sings and dances!" Mrs. Steinmetz clasped her hands to her chest, smiling at the thought of her daughter singing and dancing. "We had speakers installed all around the house so she can dance her way into any room, even the bathroom."

"What's your feeling about safety at Montgomery?" Missy asked.

"I'm concerned. Shocked that this occurred and concerned it could happen again—especially because they haven't caught the person. They have security at the doors, but no one checks for guns. You have to sign in, but that's it. Besides, this person wasn't even in the building, but at a window!" She shook her head, bewildered. "All we can do is trust the police and follow their recommendations. Beyond that, I'm trying not to think about it. I'm a little like my daughter." She smiled with a touch of embarrassment. "I watch my TV shows, read or listen to books, and just try to get through each day."

"Is your husband here?" Dora asked.

"He's working. If the Dow is open, he's there."

"The stock exchange?" Dora asked.

"That's right. We're blessed that Penelope has a great deal of ability and can, for the most part, look after herself."

"Was Penny friendly with Julian Lockhart?" Missy asked.

Mrs. Steinmetz stilled, blinking back tears. "She was—is—in love with him." A hint of her former smile returned. "She decided that about a year ago. Just came home one day and announced that she had a boyfriend and that he was a great singer. I thought she was talking about Ed Sheeran. You know, the popular singer. She's always liked his music. I didn't take her literally."

"Were any of the other boys—men—at Montgomery interested in Penny?"

"Oh yes!" The woman's smile returned in full force. "Penny's extremely popular because she's so happy, and because she loves everybody. She doesn't care about details—whether you're big, or small, any particular color, religion, or gender. She loves everyone, as long as you're nice to her. And people love her back, especially the boys!"

"Was there ever any competitiveness or animosity between the boys who might have vied for her attention?" Missy asked.

Mrs. Steinmetz didn't answer right away. She slurped her tea and said, "Hmm," several times. "Well, maybe. But I don't think it amounted to much."

Dora asked, "Do you know of anyone who might have wanted to hurt Julian Lockhart?"

"Absolutely not! He was a male version of Penelope—filled with joy, which came out as music. Of course, Penelope couldn't sing like Julian. No one could. But they were a couple of peas in a pod."

• • •

C3 wanted to hug his wife. She was, he knew, going through a challenging time at work. *The Chronicle* came out every Thursday, and to C3, it looked just fine. She had sales and graphics help, but she needed emotional support, and so at the end of many days, she collapsed into his arms, and he just held her. Sometimes she cried.

That Livvie was a comfort to them both, despite being barely a year old and having Down syndrome, C3 found astonishing.

His phone rang. Billy.

Billy was a new sponsee he'd met just yesterday at the eight o'clock meeting after the young man had courageously raised his hand and announced that he had one day back. C3 had approached him at the end of the meeting and given Billy his number, saying, "Can you call me tomorrow and not get high?"

Billy had taken his number and said, "Sure, why not?"

So, here Billy was, calling.

C3 took the call. "Hey, Billy."

"Hey, C. What's up?"

"What's up with you? Still clean?"

"You know it."

"Glad to hear it. Made a meeting yet today?"

"Not yet, but will later."

"Really?" C3 asked, wanting to be sure.

"Really."

"Said your prayers?"

"I did."

"What'd you pray for?"

"Knowledge of God's will for me and the power to carry it out," Billy said, repeating the wording of the eleventh step with the beginnings of some understanding.

"Good. Can you call me in six hours and stay clean?"

"It'll be the middle of the night, C."

"So? Did you get high in the middle of the night?"

"I'll call."

Chapter 9

Frederick Chase was a big balding man with rheumy, frightened eyes that lived behind silver wire-rimmed glasses. He wore a blue-and-white checkered shirt with a white plastic pen protector in the pocket, dark slacks, and black loafers. He opened the door with a surprised look on his face.

"Mr. Chase?" Missy said. "Dora Ellison and Missy Winters from Geller Investigations. We called ahead."

Recognition registered, and his mouth formed a nearly perfect circle. "Ohhh, yes! Come in." He stood aside, and Dora and Missy stepped past him and waited for instructions.

"Oh," Chase said again, still sounding surprised. "Let's go in here." He led the way through a set of green wooden double doors with tall glass windows and into a living room that was also green—a green velour couch, a matching green ottoman, green wooden chairs, and an old-fashioned wooden rocking chair, also painted green. The coffee table was glass with a shining metal frame. On it was a mess of papers piled several inches high.

"I'm an accountant," Chase said apologetically, "with a bunch of clients whose extensions are late." He held up a finger. "I happen to have just made a pot of coffee. How 'bout some?"

"Sure," Dora said.

Missy nodded. "Okay," she said.

Chase disappeared through the double doors. At the other end of the room was a green carpeted staircase with a green banister.

"It's like the Land of Oz in here," Missy whispered.

Dora snorted a laugh.

Chase returned, carrying a metal tray with three mugs of coffee, a small ceramic pitcher of cream, and a plate with various sweeteners. He nodded toward the coffee table. "Would you mind moving those papers to the floor? Try to keep them more or less as is, but don't worry too much about it. I know who's who in there."

Dora did as he asked, and once they all had beverages, Chase said, "So? How can I help?"

"What can you tell us about your son William's relationship with Julian Lockhart?" Dora asked.

Chase looked surprised. "He was on the stage when the shooting occurred. Surely you don't think he was somehow involved."

"We're just trying to get a complete picture of who everyone was and their relationships," Dora explained.

"William gets along with everyone. He's developmentally disabled, which to most people means he's slow. He's a big guy, but he's gentle and easygoing. He'd never hurt anyone." Chase looked down and to one side. "Unless, I suppose, they hurt him first."

"Is he friendly with Penny Steinmetz," Missy said.

"Of course." Chase chortled and smiled. "Who wouldn't like Penny Bright? I like to say he's sweet on her because sweet is the best description. William's a sweet guy when you get to know him, which isn't easy. He's extremely introverted and quiet. Fearful, in a way. He often doesn't understand what's going on around him, so he doesn't know what to say or do."

"We understand," Dora began, "that Penny was sweet on Julian Lockhart. Would that have been upsetting to William? Would he have been hurt by that fact?"

"He was unhappy about that," Chase admitted. "But William doesn't stay upset for long."

"You don't think he harbored a grudge?"

"No, I don't." Chase took his glasses off, breathed on them, and cleaned them on a napkin that had been on the coffee tray. "And frankly, I don't see the relevance, since he was standing right behind Julian when it happened. What—you think he arranged for someone to shoot Julian Lockhart? He can't arrange his clothes to get dressed in the morning."

"We didn't mean to imply that," Missy said.

Dora asked, "Were you upset that Penny cared for Julian?"

Chase laughed. "You think I killed Julian?"

"Not what I said."

"Well—do you?"

"No," Dora said.

"Are you happy with the care William is getting at Montgomery?" Missy asked.

Chase had put his glasses back on, and now he pushed them up the bridge of his nose with a middle finger. "Well, until now. My main concern is his safety. But with a shooting at an event where everyone in their care was present, how can I be confident of anything?"

"We understand," Dora said.

"No offense, but I don't see how you can. Unless you have a special child, you have no idea. Having a child at all is a wondrous thing, and having a special child is, well, special. William is such a treasure. He's big and strong, but inside he's innocent and sweet and vulnerable, and if he's at risk—" Chase took his glasses off and wiped at his eyes with the knuckles of his index fingers. "It keeps me up at night."

Dora said, "We know there are people in the neighborhood who are unhappy with the presence of Montgomery in the area. Can you think of anyone who might be angry and prone to violence?"

Chase was still for a moment, then he took a deep breath and looked at Dora with sudden clarity. "There are a group of parents who are extremely angry with Montgomery!"

• • •

Mallard and Ganderson rang the buzzer in the front foyer of the westernmost of the twin tall brick apartment buildings on the Beach City boardwalk. After being buzzed in, they took the elevator to the penthouse and rang the buzzer on one of two doorways on the floor. It was answered by a large, florid-faced woman with neck-length graying, once-blonde hair. She was wearing a yellow blouse and brown slacks.

"Detectives Mallard and Ganderson to see Mason Montgomery," Mallard said politely.

The woman didn't move. "Sharon Hurley. Mason's assistant. Badge?"

After Mallard displayed a badge, Sharon Hurley led the detectives into a sunlit room with furniture on one side and a small forest of potted plants on the other.

The fit eighty-three-year-old politician rose from the couch but didn't shake either detective's hand. "Welcome," he said, flashing his famous megawatt smile. He wore gray slacks and a matching silk polo shirt.

"Have a seat." He indicated the couch. "I don't drink coffee, but Sharon was about to bring in some tea. Can I offer you some?"

"No, thanks," Ganderson replied.

"What kind of tea?" Mallard asked.

"You don't drink tea," Ganderson muttered, but Mallard held up a hand.

"Silver Tips Imperial, imported from Darjeeling, India. We're talking elite tea," Montgomery said with an encouraging smile. "I'll have to charge you twenty bucks apiece." He chuckled. "Just kidding."

"I'll try it," Mallard said.

Ganderson shook his head, rolled his eyes, and looked away.

"There you go," Montgomery said with a grin. "Sharon, would you kindly bring us two teas?"

"Of course," Hurley said, then disappeared down the hall.

"That's some view," Mallard said, nodding toward the window. "The apartments I've been to all look directly out over the beach and board-walk, whereas yours does that but also looks west."

Montgomery's hair was perfectly styled, and he smelled of expensive cologne. "You need to come back when the sun is setting."

Hurley returned and placed a filigreed silver tray on the coffee table, then sat down in an ornate wooden armchair.

"Those are Brunello Cucinelli trousers," Mallard commented.

Montgomery was impressed. "Man knows his pants." He looked at Mallard's clothes and nodded slowly. "Brioni Brunico wool?"

"Yes, sir," Mallard said.

"And in summer. You're a man of courage."

Mallard shrugged. "Yeah, well, I make it work."

"He's a man of commando," Ganderson muttered as he leaned forward and whispered, "No underwear."

Mallard turned to his partner, raising a disapproving eyebrow, then sipped. "Wow, this is some tea!" he exclaimed.

"Imperial Silver Tip," Montgomery repeated.

Ganderson sighed. "Tell us about the Montgomery Special School."

Mason Montgomery sat down, took his teacup daintily between an index finger and thumb, and slowly sat back in his plush recliner. His face saddened. "Terrible thing." He shook his head. "A terrible, terrible thing. All of our special folks are like my own. They mean everything to me. I paid for that school to be built with my own money, and I'd hoped to keep it going, no matter what. Even after I'm gone." He continued shaking his head.

"Very generous," Ganderson observed.

Mallard continued sipping and shaking his head, not with grief but marveling at the tea's flavor.

"They're family. I have a special son, you know."

"Is he there?" Ganderson asked.

Montgomery shook his head. "He was, but he needed care that's not offered at our school. I'm considering moving him into a different wing of the facility." He shrugged. "These are hard decisions."

Ganderson leaned forward. "Do you have any idea who might be behind Julian's murder?"

Montgomery winced, shook his head, and looked at Ganderson. "Are you sure you won't have some tea?"

"Please answer the question."

"Of course not!" Sharon Hurley had sat up straight and was glaring at the detectives.

Montgomery patted the air with a palm. "Who would hurt such a magnificent, special talent? Who would hurt any of these special, special people?"

"What about you?" Ganderson asked. "Do you have any enemies? When the Lockhart boy was shot, he was standing next to you."

Hurley shook her head and made a clucking sound with her tongue.

Montgomery thought about this. "I've had a long career in politics. Many people don't like me, but that's the nature of the beast. Every issue has two sides, and the people on the other sides of the issues I've championed—or those I haven't, for that matter—tend not to like me very much, but I don't know that anyone is out to kill me. Angry, sure. But out to kill me? Still, it makes more sense than anyone wanting to kill that beautiful young man with the voice of an angel."

• • •

"Everyone at the Montgomery Special School works hard to meet the stringent standards set by the state for the care of people with special needs." Principal Claire Sumner sat opposite the two detectives with her hands primly folded on the desk in front of her. "There's a lot of accountability, a lot of evaluation. The medical personnel, teachers, aides, and caregivers are all under pressure to meet the highest quality-of-care standards—most of which are set by the state. We make sure to exceed them."

Mallard changed the subject. "What can you tell us about the school's business affairs?"

Sumner's voice faltered. "I'm not sure what you mean."

"Where does the money come from?" Ganderson asked, his tone flat.

Sumner raised her eyebrows. "From a variety of places. We receive donations. We have a successful charitable giving program. We receive grants, of course."

Ganderson continued. "Is there a single individual in charge of the incoming funds?"

"Of course, initially it came from Mr. Montgomery himself. More recently, we've had to expand our efforts, though unfortunately, not enough to remain solvent once Mr. Montgomery is gone. We have a comptroller—Virginia Rabelson. She does a wonderful job finding organizations that prepare and donate food—a program I believe that's supported via government grants, though we pay a part of the cost. Shall I put you in touch with her? Why don't I give you her contact information and tell her she can expect to hear from you?"

"Please do that."

Much of the rest of the afternoon was devoted to research, as Ganderson and Mallard decided to build up a list of Mason Montgomery's relationships and checked up on the information provided by the Montgomery School's office prior to calling Virginia Rabelson.

Chapter 10

As always, Sarah spent her work hours juggling caring for Livvie, working on stories, and vetting her stringers' information. Today, she had answered five editorial-related calls since three o'clock, and all five had been about the murder of Julian Lockhart—four from parents of young people at Montgomery. All had called before. What could she tell them? She wanted to point them to yesterday's story about the bank robbery at one of Beach City's main banks—a robbery that Beach City's finest had quickly solved. She wondered if Claire Sumner was nudging parents to reach out to the paper in the hopes that *The Chronicle* would somehow put pressure on the police to find the murderer, or at least a scapegoat, for the death of Julian Lockhart. Perhaps these same people were pressuring the police too.

She had perused several local Beach City and moms' Facebook groups and seen that some of the parents of local people with special needs at Montgomery were clamoring for more to be done to maintain safety, both at Montgomery and locally in general. The clamoring had coalesced into a plan; a meeting was planned for three days in the future, Saturday afternoon, at three o'clock in the back room of Mae's Diner for anyone who wished to attend so that people could voice their concerns and find a way forward.

She had three other stories to edit, two to write, and artwork and ads to approve. Lemieux and Esther were similarly overburdened. She groaned—she'd forgotten this week's pay, which was to have been covered by bank deposits this morning.

Livvie started to cry.

"Be right there, honey!" she called and began composing letters to her employees and contractors, telling them that their money would be a day late this week. Again.

Livvie's cries turned to shrieks; when it came to diaper changes, her daughter wasn't patient. "I know," Sarah said. "Diaper rash sucks."

"What's for dinner?" C3 had come in. She heard the apartment door slam shut behind him.

"Would you change Livvie, darling? Got my hands full."

His blond head peeked into the room. "Can't, babe. Greasy hands." He waved his hands at her; they were indeed filthy. She exhaled as Livvie increased the volume of her cries.

"So wash them," Sarah muttered. She paused, listening, and when she was sure he wasn't going to change Livvie, she got up and changed her daughter's diaper. She then opened her *Chronicle* financial spreadsheet and scanned the upcoming bills, then opened a second window showing the balance of *The Chronicle*'s business bank account, and a third showing *The Chronicle*'s line of credit. She looked from one to the other to the other—from money owed, to cash on hand, to available credit. She double-checked, her breath coming fast, a hollowness squeezing her chest; sweat ran down her sides.

She leaned forward on her elbows and covered her face with her palms. Even if she rescinded Lemieux's and Esther's well-deserved pay raises, she wasn't going to make payroll, again. And she wasn't going to be able to pay her creditors, again—creditors who'd told her that there wasn't going to be a next time.

She thought of C3, who was so proud of her that he babbled to everyone he met about his wife the journalist-inheritor of the local newspaper—a successful writer and businesswoman. He knew she was in over her head and had suggested several times that she find help, particularly because she was raising Livvie while running *The Chronicle* from home.

Her reaction had been stark refusal. She could do both, and she didn't want some stranger in the house purporting to take care of their daughter—a daughter with special needs. How would they find and vet such a person? But the question was moot—she wasn't going to do it.

Well, now her back was against the wall. She saw that she couldn't possibly go on—that she wasn't the superwoman she made herself out to be and couldn't run *The Chronicle*'s business affairs while being Livvie's full-time mom. She would have to run the "closing our doors" editorial and declare bankruptcy.

She closed her eyes and breathed in slowly for a count of four, held her breath for a count of four, then exhaled for a count of four. She did this several times, pausing between each series of breaths for a count of four—box breathing.

An idea came to her. She took out her phone and dialed the one person she'd been absolutely certain she would never ask for help—and yet the only person she felt she could turn to, given the circumstances.

• • •

By two forty-five on Saturday afternoon, the back room at Mae's Diner was already full. Chairs and tables had been stacked in the rear of the room so that a half dozen motorized wheelchairs and their occupants could sit comfortably along one wall. Parents of all ages—from mid-twenties through early seventies—filled the chairs at the tables around the room; others stood quietly, arms folded across their chests, or held notebooks and pens, or cell phones with cameras or open documents ready to be filled with notes about the proceedings.

Claire Sumner stood at the front of the crowd, her hands clasped neatly behind her back, her sensible shoes drawn together. She was ready.

A woman stood and clapped three times. She was in her early fifties, conservatively dressed, with small green eyes and graying hair that was neatly arranged in a style that had been out of fashion for at least forty years. Rachel Torson was the president of the local chapter of SEPTA—Special Education PTA—and she was a force to be reckoned with. Once the room quieted, she sat down and spoke to the principal.

"Going forward, what can you do to assure us that our loved ones will be safe at Montgomery?"

Principal Sumner gave a quick nod to acknowledge the question. "First, let me say that we're all brokenhearted and deeply, deeply concerned, while at the same time determined and literally shot out of a cannon when it comes to shoring up the security at Montgomery."

Torson snorted quietly and turned to a woman sitting beside her—a pale woman with yellow hair, dark glasses, and an intensely focused, rodent-like expression—with small eyes and a twitching nose. "Literally shot out of a cannon? I think not!"

The rodent-woman smiled as though she understood the comment, then turned to Sumner, and asked, "But what have you *done*?"

Principal Sumner took a deep breath. "We've met several times with the police and gone over everything we know that occurred on … when … at that time." She struggled, unable to verbalize the tragedy.

"And what have the police done?" asked a man in a New York Mets cap, curly brown hair spilling from its back and front.

"They've advised us to add armed security guards at all entrances, whom we're in the process of vetting and which we'll do. They've also advised us to increase the number of video cameras around the grounds and inside our building. We're doing that as well."

A heavy woman in a too-tight starched white blouse and white parachute pants with blue stripes down the sides raised her hand. "Is it true that the area outside the auditorium, the area from which the shots came, wasn't covered by your security cameras?"

Sumner pressed her lips together and nodded. "Unfortunately, that's the case, but that's being remedied."

"I have to tell you," said a tall, black-haired man with the weathered features of someone who spent a great deal of time out of doors, "the powers that be seem to have it in for our families. You've got one job—keep us safe—and you're not doing it! You've failed! I mean, face it! It's the people in charge—they're the problem." He turned toward the crowd. "How do you think my son ended up on the spectrum in the first place? Vaccinations!" He shook his head and stabbed the air with a finger as he turned toward the beleaguered principal. "The people in charge!"

A young woman with biscuit-colored hair, wearing an orange top and blue jeans, shook her head. "I'm not sure I want my daughter to continue at Montgomery after this tragedy. It seems to me that you've demonstrated that you can't keep our loved ones safe, and for me—that's a deal breaker!"

The weather-beaten man had sat down, but now he stood up again. "Maybe you ought to think about resigning and making room for someone who runs a tighter ship! How 'bout that?"

• • •

The morning light slanted through the living room window, making yellow-white puddles on the carpet. Missy lay back with her head on a pillow, her iPad propped up on her belly, resting against her thighs. She was doing a *sudoku* at expert level, and she'd gone as far as she could without asking the program for a hint, which she was loath to do. She closed the iPad and laid it down on her chest. Taking a break from a *sudoku* often allowed her mind to work on the problem in the background while she did other things, and when she returned to the puzzle, the log-jam would sometimes be cleared.

"I'm having trouble getting past it," she said. "Who would shoot a kid with cerebral palsy?"

Dora was working on her own puzzle, the traditional, visual kind—an image printed on cardboard and cut into dozens of tiny pieces that had to be fitted together again. She looked up, took her enormous "Football Giants Eli Manning" mug in her fist, and slurped at her still-hot java. "A sicko—plain and simple."

"Agreed," Missy said. "So how do you catch a sicko who murders people with special needs?"

Dora raised an eyebrow and slurped more coffee. She adored coffee and believed it helped her think, despite Missy's admonition that the coffee was merely a stimulant. Dora suspected coffee was infused with spiritual powers that went far beyond the beans. "If this is as simple and random as a sicko killing someone who has special needs, I'd say it might be a perfect—if really fucked-up—crime. But I don't think it is. I don't think it ever is. This particular sicko had a reason—a twisted, crazy reason—but to his or her mind, a reason. We just have to find it."

"Meaning, we have to think like this sicko."

Dora pointed at Missy. "Exactly." She walked to a stained wooden cabinet that had three drawers on its front. The middle of the three drawers had a keyhole in the center. Dora took her keys from a plate that was next to the door to the hallway, found the right key, and unlocked the drawer. "Need to show you something."

She slid the drawer open and held up a small black pistol. "This is a Glock 42."

"Whoa," Missy breathed. "Do you have a license for that thing?"

Dora nodded. "Applied for it when I was with the academy. Was approved for it once we started working for Adam, who helped me finalize it. C'mon. I need to show you how it works."

"Why? I don't have a license. Besides, don't you just aim and shoot?"

"Hang on. Look, you'll probably never use it, but in an emergency … Well, it's good to know." She laid the little gun in her hand and held it out. It fit comfortably in her palm. "This is a semiautomatic pistol."

She put the gun down on the counter, took a rectangular black magazine and some cartridges from the drawer, and laid them on the counter next to the Glock. "You load the magazine by holding each cartridge be-tween your thumb and forefinger like this, and press the back of the car-tridge firmly into the front of the magazine. It'll snap into place. Then you press the second cartridge down on the front of the first one. If you find it difficult to hold the magazine in your hand, you can set it on a flat surface, so you have a strong base when you press down. With each one, after pressing down, you slide it back. Once you've got your cartridges in place, tap the magazine against the palm of your other hand." Dora demonstrated. "Make sure the cartridges are seated firmly. Then you slide the cartridge into the stock of the gun, where it will snap in place—and you can jiggle it a little to make sure it's firm. Now, to use the gun, you've got to chamber a round. You'll need to pull the slide back and then forward. I think the best way to do this is to lay the palm of your hand over the slide and pull back while pushing forward on the stock, then let the slide snap forward—and you've got a round in the chamber." She demonstrated. "Now you try."

After several diffident attempts, Missy was able to successfully load the magazine and chamber a round.

"What about shooting it?" Missy asked.

"Very easy." Dora showed Missy how to wrap her fingers around the stock, with her forefinger outside the trigger guard. "I highly recom-mend a two-handed grip. Simply square your stance, bring your other hand up, and fold it over your right hand, to steady it and give it support."

After another ten minutes, Dora was confident that Missy would be able to use the Glock, should the need arise.

• • •

Less than one mile away, in an unfinished concrete basement below a two-story home, a twenty-seven-year-old man with long brown hair, a beard, a mustache, and a week's worth of stubble was taking apart a rifle.

His name was Richard Dubon, but he was known locally as Lonny because his most recent and longest-term employment had been as an enforcer for loan sharks. Originally, his nickname had been "Loany," and over time and through usage it had become Lonny. Another change that had occurred over time was that his specialty was now murder—not something he'd ever aspired to do. He'd simply gotten in way over his head with the wrong people; he'd griped, moaned, lied, and bitched his way to owing more and more money until he had no choice but to run, become a victim, or earn his way out of trouble doing things no one else wanted to do. The choice had been easy. He'd always been quick with his fists and rather enjoyed hurting people, having been hurt himself more than a few times. He had a sadistic streak, which he fed at every opportunity. If asked why, he might have said, "Hey, it feels good!"

He was also a talented thief—a guy who'd gotten by as he'd grown up by stealing from the homes of his friends. He had a long history of getting himself into trouble and fighting his way out of it.

But Lonny Dubon had eventually sunk deeper into criminality because he'd never been willing or able to earn a living on the right side of the law. He also had a taste for cocaine, which was expensive, and which was fronted to him—as long as he was willing to pay or earn his way out of debt.

Lonny also had a special skill that set him apart from other local muscle: he was an expert sniper. He came by his sniping skills genetically; his father had been a marine sniper in Vietnam. The skill had enabled Lonny to become an enforcer of choice for loan sharks in Nassau County and western Queens.

At the moment, he was nervous, so he was doing what calmed him: taking apart and putting together his baby, a Ruger Precision Gen 3 Bolt-Action Rifle—a sniper's dream.

He'd done what he'd been told: used .338 Lapua Magnum rounds, which had been specifically developed as long-range marine sniping rounds that could penetrate body armor at over a half mile at nearly three thousand feet per second.

With one shot he had, so he'd been told, now canceled all of his debt. But he was worried; so much of his debt had personal grievances attached—grievances that came from dangerous people, some of whom had long and nasty memories.

And so he took the rifle apart, laid the pieces neatly on the old wooden workbench, took exactly three deep breaths, and put it together again. Over and over and over.

• • •

Sarah and Livvie looked at each other for a long moment; Sarah hoped that her daughter felt for her even a fraction of the adoration and joy she felt for her daughter. Almost immediately though, her joy was replaced by foreboding as she thought of the fact that, though a few weeks beyond her first birthday, Livvie was neither walking nor exhibiting any of the pre-walking behaviors Sarah had hoped for. When she was sitting on the floor near a table or chair, Livvie didn't attempt to pull herself to a standing position; the idea didn't appear to occur to her. She rarely crawled and took little interest in her blocks, play sets, or toddler learning toys. Sarah and C3 had expected slow progress, but living through it was painful and frightening.

Livvie was watching her from her car seat, a removable system that allowed her to sit in her own cushioned armchair on the floor in their apartment while Sarah worked. Sarah wondered if Livvie was aware of her anxiety and if her worry was hurting her daughter. Whenever she realized she was worried about worrying, she knew it was time to get back to work.

She decided to write a guest editorial in this week's *Chronicle*. So she brought the file up on her MacBook and began working on it. She noted that people had been demonizing the staff and administration at the Montgomery Special School—an unfortunate knee-jerk reaction to Julian's murder. The families of the special people Montgomery served had every right to be angry, of course, and Sarah wrote that the editorial staff at *The Chronicle* understood their pain and fear. But this tragedy wasn't, in *The Chronicle*'s opinion, caused by Montgomery's administration—and that included any neglect on their part. Some suggested that changes at Montgomery were in order. In Sarah's, and therefore *The Chronicle*'s, opinion, the most productive focus for the Montgomery community ought to be healing. Families and staff alike were traumatized and understandably fearful for the future. Who was behind this horrific crime? Were others at risk? What steps could be taken at Montgomery to ensure their community's safety?

The only way to address these concerns was for the community at Montgomery to unite, for the Beach City community to stand with Montgomery and say no to violence and terror, and for the police to do everything in their power to make sure Montgomery and all of Beach City was a safe place for everyone, including and especially the city's special residents.

• • •

Dora and Missy were at their new desks going over the Lockhart case notes, while Adam Geller sat at his desk with his chair facing the back of the room, watching yet another episode of the old TV show *The Odd Couple.*

"I wonder if every community has locals like ours who don't want people with special needs around," Missy said to Dora while looking at her notes.

Dora's mouth twisted. "And if one of them is a sociopath, I'm still at a loss as to how to think like one."

"Me too," Missy said. "Um, so are you still pissed at Christine and Charlie for not inviting us to their party?"

Dora looked back at Missy for a long moment. "Are you conflating me being pissed about our non-invitation with sociopathic thinking?"

Missy looked stunned. "Whoa! Where'd *that* come from?"

Dora glared back at Missy. "Well?"

"No!"

Dora's tone changed to one of sadness. "Look, people say or do shit, and sometimes it gets to me. Like Charlie and Christine having that party and not inviting us, and then not reaching out to apologize when they realized it's hurtful."

"Dor," Missy said gently, "I think you're making too much of it."

"Or Sarah and C3. They were at the party. Why are we not hearing from them?"

Missy let out a breath. "Well, why are they not hearing from us?" She reached forward and tried to touch Dora's arm, but Dora pulled away.

"Fuck, never mind." Dora shook her head, still scowling. "And why hasn't Vanessa asked me to watch her kids?"

"Dor, maybe she has other stuff going on. I suspect that none of these people are behaving in whatever ways they're behaving because they want to hurt you."

Dora thought about this and raised an eyebrow. "Well …"

The office phone rang. "Geller Investigations," Thelma brayed from the front of the office. She was silent for a moment. "A Fred Chase on line one," she squawked.

Dora took the call. "Hi, Mr. Chase. This is Dora Ellison."

"Something occurred to me, and I thought it made sense to give you a call."

"What's that?"

"There's a group of families who are really angry at Montgomery."

"I know. We're seeing it on Facebook and in *The Chronicle*."

"No. This is different. These families are angry at Mason Montgomery, personally. It's been going on for a while, and it's related to something specific. People are enraged, and the spearhead of the group, the angriest among them, is Julian's grandfather, Jack Ashford."

When she ended the call, Dora looked at Missy for a long moment. Missy raised an eyebrow with an "and?" expression. Then Dora called Ashford, explained that she and Missy were investigators, and asked if they might stop by.

Ashford agreed.

• • •

Dora and Missy approached the sprawling Victorian bay-front home, and Missy rang the bell.

"Beautiful view," Dora mused. Beyond the home's yard and dock, two large sailboats could be seen inching along the channel. A fishing charter had dropped anchor, and a dozen fishermen had their lines in the water, hoping for keeper fluke. A half dozen gulls circled noisily overhead.

Jack Ashford answered his door.

"Hi, Mr. Ashford," Missy began. "I'm Missy Winters, and this is Dora Ellison. We're with Geller Investigations. Do you have a few minutes to speak with us?"

The elderly man gave a tired smile, nodded, and beckoned them inside. "How can I help?" Ashford asked once they were seated in the living room. "I've already met with police detectives."

"We're interested in learning more about the Montgomery School."

Ashford's eyes widened. "What would you like to know?"

"Your impression of the school."

"That covers a lot of ground." Ashford paused, and a crease appeared on his forehead. "And if you'd asked a month ago, I'd have said the only thing that mattered was Julian's safety." He gave a rueful shrug. "I don't know that I can blame the school for the actions of some nutcase, but obviously the security on the grounds ought to have been better. Not much I can do but leave that to the police and Claire Sumner." He glanced from Missy to Dora. "Do you have any ideas as to how someone with a gun got themselves outside that auditorium, who that person might be, or why they would do such a thing?"

"Well," said Dora carefully. "We can't comment on an ongoing investigation."

Ashford's brows drew together. "Really? You're not cops."

Dora looked Ashford in the eye. "To give you a straight answer, Mr. Ashford—no, we don't know, but we're working on it."

One corner of the elderly man's mouth turned up. "Thank you."

Missy glanced at Dora, who continued to look directly at Ashford. "What's your opinion of Mason Montgomery?" Missy asked.

Ashford had cast his eyes downward, retreating into his thoughts, but now his eyes snapped to Dora. "Why would you ask me that?"

"Well, to be honest, word has it that you're not too happy with the man."

Ashford took a deep breath, and the man seemed to change, to grow in stature, the wrinkles around his eyes and mouth smoothing, his brow lowering, his gaze hardening. "The man's a travesty," Ashford snarled. "He had this school, a wonderful place, built and funded. There isn't another facility anywhere near here with the quality of care—the quality of life—that the Montgomery School and Montgomery Care offer to special people like Julian. The love Montgomery has for his son shines through in the care offered by his facility."

Missy asked, "Then why are you upset with him?"

"I'll tell you why. Montgomery has consistently said—no, guaranteed—that his facility would continue, and that those in his facility's care would have an ongoing high quality of life, even after he was gone. In perpetuity!" He angrily emphasized the last word.

"Did he mean he would put that in his will?" Dora asked.

"That's exactly what he meant! He didn't just mean it. He said it. And a lot of people heard him say it. I'm not the only one who feels this way. Those were his words! He guaranteed it, and he reneged, and by doing so, he put many, many special lives at risk!" Ashford sat up straighter. His chin came up. "I would have thought that a man like Montgomery, with his own special child, would understand the importance of quality, ongoing care."

Ashford's jaw was clenched, and he was breathing heavily, glaring with growing, barely contained rage. "What do you think becomes of special young people after their parents, or grandparents in Julian's case, are gone? Who will care for them? The state? Ha! You wouldn't want to see anyone, including your worst enemy, in the state's care! That man … that man, Montgomery, built an oasis, a fantastic different sort of institution—one in whose care we could truly trust our loved ones for the rest of their lives—and then he pulled it out from under us all! He put so many, so many special lives at risk! I'm an old man! Who would have looked after Julian after I'm gone, which isn't so far off? I'll tell you who—nobody!"

"What about your daughter?" Missy offered.

The anger seeped from Ashford's face, and he was left deflated and sad. "She can't. She signed away her rights when she gave him to me, to protect him from being hurt because she wasn't capable of caring for him."

"What about Julian's father?" Dora asked.

Jack Ashford turned to Dora, eyes again blazing, boring into her. When he spoke, his words weren't so much spoken as hurled—a single incendiary syllable. "No!"

A few minutes later, once they were safely in Dora's turbo, Dora commented. "I think Ashford's a little unhinged."

Missy turned to Dora. "I hate to ask this, but isn't it a little convenient for Ashford that Julian's future is no longer a worry?"

•••

"It's a great day at The Bernelli Group, Beach City's premier ad agency. How may I direct your call?"

Despite her anxiety, Sarah had to smile. "Hi, Michele. It's Sarah Turner at *The Chronicle*. Is Charlie around?"

"He is, but he's on a call. Did you want to wait?"

"Please." While she waited, Sarah wondered if she really wanted to share her stress, overwhelm, and what she saw as her business failures with a man with whom she nearly always disagreed and whom she believed to be a terrible influence on her fiancé—a man who was a wedding ring away from being her father-in-law, and very likely an active alcoholic who had little interest in changing that status. Did she want that level of enmeshment with a man of such questionable judgment?

Apparently she did, because when Charlie came on the line, Sarah told him all about her struggles to run her online newspaper, which was losing money at a time when stories critical to the public welfare were daily happenings, and all while doing her best to raise a special little girl —a girl who happened to be Charlie's granddaughter.

At the very least, she'd expected a lecture from Charlie, who was so often overwrought and at least a little buzzed, if not three sheets to the wind. He was a man whose politics she abhorred, and yet he was a man she respected as a successful businessman, despite frowning on some of his business tactics. There was no arguing with success.

But what she got surprised her. Charlie simply said, "I have an idea. Let me see what I can do," and ended the call. She didn't even have a chance to ask about Christine's pregnancy.

Sarah put on her favorite satellite rock station and listened to a mix of her favorite bands. Fifteen minutes later, her phone rang.

"*Chronicle*—this is Sarah."

"Sarah, my name is LaChance Williams. I just had a call from Charlie Bernelli about your situation, and I think I might be able to help. C3 knows me too."

Sarah thought to ask how LaChance knew C3, but then it came to her, and she chose not to bring it up.

LaChance went on. "Anyway, I've been looking for something to invest in, and I think a community newspaper might be just the thing. I love Beach City. It's been my home all my life—and this might be a way for me to contribute to the well-being of my hometown, while perhaps giving you a hand with some of the business aspects of your newspaper."

· · ·

Ganderson read the memo on his screen, sat back, and whistled, then addressed his partner. "Re-Morse put together a list of confiscated firearms from the last two and a half months." He was talking about Lieutenant Gary "Re" Morse, the obsessive-compulsive clerk who worked the Beach City Police Department's front desk and handled many of the mundane details the department regularly required.

"Let's hear it," Mallard replied.

"We've got handguns that include Berettas, Colts, Heckler & Kochs, Pindads, Rugers, SIG Sauers, Smith & Wessons, and Walthers. How's that? Now, the rifles include Brownings, Remingtons, Springfields, Winchesters, and a bunch of AR-15s."

"We oughta have our own trade show," Mallard mused. "Bet it would attract a crowd."

"Yeah, and we'd catch a bunch of perps. These numbers are a significant increase from previous years," Ganderson emphasized.

After a pause, both detectives refocused on their computer screens. Then Mallard's cell phone rang. He pulled it from his pocket and looked to see who was calling.

"Uh-oh," he said and took the call. "Hello, Kay." He listened. "An eye doctor appointment? Why can't you drive yourself?" He paused. "Uh-huh. Well, it's very responsible of you to ask rather than drive if you're sure you can't pass a breathalyzer, but wouldn't it make sense to wait until after the appointment to have your first drink of the day?"

Ganderson laughed quietly, watching his partner. Mallard shook his head and pointed to his phone, then held out his hand helplessly.

"Well, why not a taxi? Okay, so you don't— What about an Uber? Well, they vet the drivers, Kay! Besides, you're in no position to—" He gave a loud sigh. "Okay, okay! I'll be there in fifteen. Hey!" he shouted. "That's the best I can do, and no, I'm not running lights and sirens for your damn eye doctor appointment. Don't tell me not to curse! Aw, hell!" He ended the call and looked at Ganderson as he stood up to leave. "What are you laughing at?"

Ganderson waved a hand and went back to his computer. Several minutes later, he noticed an internal message from Lieutenant Trask flagged for "GG," short for "the Goose and the Gander," the detectives' unofficial, sometimes fond sometimes not so fond, nicknames within the precinct. He opened the message and read it:

"Got something related to the Lockhart case. Please see me."

He got up and walked to Trask's desk, but she continued to work as though he weren't there.

"What do you have for us, Cathy?"

She continued working, ignoring him.

"Hey!" he snapped. "I'm talking to you!"

No answer.

He slammed his hand down on her desk and was satisfied to see her jump in her seat. "You've got something on a live case, and you won't give it to me because of your stupid, petty, shit games? This is a fucking homicide!"

She was suddenly blinking back tears and shaking her head. Her brown hair, which had been tied in a bun, came down and whirled around her head. This stopped him; he'd touched that hair and slid it between his fingers. Somehow, her intransigence turned him on. Before she could see the evidence, he turned quickly and hurried into the men's room, one of several individual bathrooms that formed a row in a hallway just off the department's front entrance. He sat down in the stall to sulk with his pants still up, his face in his hands. Someone banged on the door.

"Occupied!" he yelled.

The banging came again.

"Hey!" he snarled.

"It's me." It was Cathy Trask's voice, and she sounded upset. Ganderson opened the door a crack. She forced her way inside, closed the door, and locked it behind her. She took his face between her hands, bent, and kissed him—hard. She reached down and felt that he was already erect. Then she dropped her pants, stepped out of them, took him in her hand, and guided him into her.

Then she opened her shirt, sat on his lap with his face between her breasts, and bounced.

• • •

Later, when Mallard returned, he sat down at his computer, read the message on his screen, and looked at Ganderson.

"Virginia Rabelson, the Montgomery comptroller, is somehow linked to Maverick Lockhart and money laundering?" Mallard asked.

Ganderson nodded but said nothing.

"And you got this from Trask?"

Ganderson nodded again.

"How?"

Ganderson looked at him and smiled a crocodile smile. "I asked. Nicely. Very nicely."

Mallard's eyes widened. "Fuck's sake!"

Chapter 11

LaChance drew up an agreement that Sarah amended several times, and they both signed it. He would be a 49 percent owner of *The Chronicle,* with Sarah being majority owner. He would infuse *The Chronicle* with enough funding to pay its obligations for two years and oversee advertising, finances, and payroll, while Sarah would handle reportage, editorial, and creative. She would also oversee the technological workings of their online newspaper or delegate those responsibilities as she saw fit—likely to Lemieux, who was her resident techie—but would hand off purchases and upgrades to LaChance, with Lemieux acting as consultant. They would discuss and do their best to mutually agree on all policies and major decisions, with Sarah having final say on all.

The immediate effect of the arrangement was one of immense relief for Sarah. Her days opened up with time and energy she could spend with Livvie and C3 while giving the reportage, writing, and editing aspects of *The Chronicle*—the news—the attention it deserved.

Their love life was suddenly and vigorously renewed as her stress level was reduced and she and C3 had the time and inclination for intimacy.

The Chronicle's daily workings were instantly less stressful because LaChance encouraged her to bring on two additional stringer reporters and a new reporter-typesetter-designer. Best of all, LaChance himself was a source of positivity, business experience, knowledge, and information—not to mention goodwill. Sarah congratulated herself on the decision and made a point of thanking Charlie, her de facto father-in-law and benefactor, for the connection.

The only downside, if it was in fact a downside, was C3. LaChance, C3 explained to Sarah, was his sponsor, and he was a bit uncomfortable with his sponsor being his wife's business partner. Sarah said she understood and asked how serious his discomfort was. C3 claimed it was "not a big deal," and Sarah said she would take care not to tread on C3's recovery in any way.

Still, a small seed of doubt about *The Chronicle*'s new backer sprouted in Sarah's mind.

• • •

Ganderson pressed the buzzer while Mallard took in their surroundings. Though the building was only two blocks from the ocean, the neighborhood was decidedly not one of Beach City's nicest. The strip of grass along the street was overgrown with weeds, as was a driveway. The outside door's paint was peeling. Garbage was strewn around the building's grounds.

Once inside, Mallard looked around the slovenly lobby for an elevator and, seeing none, gazed up the stairway, then at Ganderson. He sighed. The building was a four-floor walk-up.

Ganderson said nothing and took the lead up the stairs.

The woman who opened the door to the apartment looked to Mallard like a meth head; she was bony and shriveled, yet likely possessed of the wiry strength so many meth heads displayed when cornered.

"Cops?" she said, confirming what to her was obvious.

Ganderson held up his badge.

"Might be better if we spoke inside," Mallard suggested.

"Warrant?"

"Didn't think we'd need one," Ganderson answered. "Unless you've got something to hide."

Diana Moran laughed, and Mallard could see that she was missing several teeth.

"Nice try," she cackled. "Might be better if we talk right here."

"Okay," Ganderson said in an "it's your funeral" tone. "We're here about the young man who was murdered at the Montgomery School."

"That *special* young man," she said sarcastically. "I figured."

"Why did you figure that?" Ganderson continued.

"Just ask your questions."

"Okay," Mallard said. "What were you doing outside the auditorium at the time of the shooting?"

"What?"

"The shot that killed Julian Lockhart originated from the area outside the auditorium—an area where you were witnessed walking at the approximate time of the shooting."

"Witnessed? Who witnessed me?" Moran demanded to know. "Don't I get to confront my accuser?"

"Do you deny you were there?" Ganderson shot back.

She didn't answer directly. "I *will* tell you what I saw as I was leaving the building."

"By the entrance in the hallway adjacent to the auditorium," Ganderson finished for her.

But Moran continued looking at Mallard. "I saw a man with an implement."

"An implement?" Mallard repeated. "What does that mean?"

"I didn't see it up close. But it was long and like a cylinder."

"Like a rifle?" Mallard asked.

She shrugged. "I don't know much about rifles. Or rakes, for that matter." She laughed. "I thought it was a rake. I thought he was a groundskeeper."

"And this was outside the auditorium during the performance?" Mallard asked.

Moran nodded. "Yup."

"So, you were there." Ganderson accused.

She nodded. "I left as the performances—if you can call them that—started. I didn't want to see that crap. I can't stand that school or its *special* people." She twisted the word scornfully.

Ganderson asked, "Can you describe this guy you say you saw?"

"He was dark-skinned, but he was a white guy—with sort of dark skin. And he had long brown hair. Was probably in his thirties. Had a beard and mustache. He got out of a green car—maybe an Impala or a Taurus. Your basic green car. And he passed me. We passed each other."

"You were leaving the school, and he was heading toward it with this implement," Mallard said.

"That's right. Got any other questions?"

"That's it," said Mallard, with a look at Ganderson.

"For now," Ganderson added.

Diana Moran slammed the door. They heard the bolt snap into place.

• • •

"Rags to riches," Mallard said when they entered Maverick Lockhart's building. Once Lockhart led them inside his opulent apartment, Mallard gave a low whistle.

"Nice place," he said.

"Thank you," Lockhart replied. "Please, have a seat."

"You didn't have custody of Julian," Ganderson began. He smoothed back his hair, then took a handkerchief out of a pants pocket and wiped the hair product from his hands.

"I did at first. After Emily gave him up, I mean. Briefly, when he was little. But I have business interests. I travel. I couldn't give Julian the attention he needed. I couldn't have, even if he'd been a normal kid."

"You think your son was abnormal?" Mallard asked, his eyebrows raised.

"Look, I don't always say the politically correct thing, but the truth is, Julian had a condition—several, in fact—that weren't normal. He couldn't do things other kids could do, and he needed help most kids wouldn't need. My life is very tied up in my businesses, and I couldn't give the boy what he needed. Isn't it better to admit that than be there with him and do a shitty job? Wouldn't that be selling him short?"

The room was briefly silent.

"Fair enough," said Mallard.

"Can you please explain," Ganderson probed, "how it is that your business interests are somehow tied up with Virginia Rabelson, the Montgomery School's comptroller? And why the receipts from your restaurants—the volume of cash flowing through them, and some other business interests you apparently have—don't match the business they do?"

Maverick Lockhart sat back, smiling broadly, his right arm thrown over his sofa's backrest. "What do you say we order out for lunch? Sounds like you guys might be staying awhile. If I'll be explaining the inner workings of my businesses to you, the least I can do is feed you." He laughed.

Ganderson remained impassive. "Just answer the question."

"Well, that's several questions. And why not join me in a bite to eat?"

"I'll tell you why," Ganderson said. "I break bread with my friends, and you're not my friend."

"Aww," Lockhart feigned sorrow and grinned at Mallard while pointing at Ganderson. "He's not my friend." He feigned an overly sad expression.

"Answer the question," Ganderson repeated.

"Questions," Lockhart said, emphasizing the plural. "First answer, I have no idea who the woman you're mentioning is. Could it be someone who works at Julian's school is connected with one of my businesses? Sure. I have diverse and varied interests. Second answer, sounds like you're accusing me of money laundering. If you are," he held out both his hands, "go ahead and arrest me. But you can't because I'm not involved in money laundering. My restaurants have been audited. I know most of the local IRS agents by name. Many businesses I'm involved with have been audited. Some haven't. Some've been audited more than once. Know what they found? Nothing."

Having learned all they could, the detectives returned to the car. Ganderson glanced at Mallard. "If he was audited, which I doubt, and they didn't find anything, which I doubt." His eyes widened, his eyebrows waggled, and he rubbed his fingers together in the universal sign for graft.

As Ganderson started the car, Mallard's cell phone rang. He looked at the number and muttered, "Trask," then took the call. "What've you got, Cathy?" He listened, then hung up and looked at Ganderson. "Info on the bullet that was pulled off the Montgomery stage."

"And?"

"Armor-piercing AP485, 16.1 grams," Mallard said.

"Likely a .338 Lapua Magnum," Ganderson mused, as he put the car into gear, drove to the corner, and turned left onto Beach City's main road.

"What does that tell us?" Mallard's question was rhetorical.

Ganderson thought for a moment. "Those are marksman's rounds. Hard to believe that whoever did the shooting didn't hit what he was aiming at."

Mallard agreed. "He … or she."

Chapter 12

Sarah held Livvie up to the mobile and blew gently on the colorful hanging plastic animals, but Livvie seemed to look right through them toward the wall on the opposite side of the room. Her eyes wandered but never alighted on any one object.

Sarah sighed and held her daughter against her chest, one palm covering Livvie's warm, fragrant hair, into which she burrowed her nose.

In one of her *Chronicle* inboxes, she'd noticed an email from someone with the initials A. K. who was suggesting that the certifying process at schools or facilities for people with special needs ought to be changed at the state or perhaps federal level to plug holes of the sort that had allowed for the murder of Julian Lockhart.

Two emails below was a message from LaChance saying that he'd seen and loved that email and suggesting she do whatever she could to fan any flames or embers it might cause. The greater the outcry about the murder at Montgomery, the better for *The Chronicle*. More outcry equaled more eyeballs on ads. Clients, LaChance emphasized, would love this! He continued, "Perhaps we ought to editorialize that the principal be replaced?"

• • •

Luis and Joan, the part-timer Charlie had brought in for the project, had completed forty alternate versions of Benny's Bar graphics, and Vanessa was reasonably confident that Charlie would approve of the work—at least until Ben Schucker destroyed it. She had little control over Charlie's codependency issues with clients, so she knew she had to let that go.

Vanessa had spent little time on the work at hand tonight; instead, she'd googled "autism spectrum disorder" and sifted through the results, comparing her findings with Buster's lethargy. The results terrified her, which led to more frantic googling, hunting, scrutinizing, and, ultimately, freaking out. *How is it possible*, she wondered, *that happy, engaged, and oh-so-smart Buster is now on the spectrum?*

She arrived home to find Kelvin sitting on the couch with his phone on the backrest, next to his ear. He was listening to music.

"Why is that there?" she asked, indicating the phone.

"I want to hear if one of the boys wakes up, so I didn't want to use earbuds."

She sat down beside him. "What are you listening to?"

Kelvin reached back, took his phone from atop the backrest, and looked at it. Then he held it out for Vanessa to see.

"Brown Bird, 'End of Days,'" she read. "Put it back on."

Kelvin did, placing the phone on his knee, then he and Vanessa sat back on the couch and closed their eyes, listening.

"It's so sad," she murmured when the song concluded. "And yet it's beautiful."

Kelvin opened his eyes. "Exactly—like life. Brutal, but you've got to seek and find the beauty."

"I'm so freaked out about Buster."

Neither of them spoke for a moment. Finally, Kelvin asked, "Have you brought him to a doctor yet?"

Vanessa shook her head and bit her lower lip. "I'm afraid to. I wouldn't know where to go. I don't know who to trust."

"I can get you some names," Kelvin assured her. "From work."

"I can't see ever sending him to Montgomery, given what happened there." She was silent for a moment, then asked, "Do you think someone's killing people with special needs?" Vanessa's face reflected the fear in her voice.

Kelvin shook his head. "I don't know what that was about. I have to trust that between the school and the cops, they'll figure it out. At least Buster's not there now. Anyway, I'll bet one of the doctors on my list can help you figure out what's going on with him."

"What did he do tonight?"

"He played a little with his blocks. He lines them up a certain way, then knocks them down. He did that over and over. He did scream a little, but not too much. Drew and I are working on a surprise for you."

Vanessa smiled and touched Kelvin's hand. "Thank you."

• • •

Dora was at the coffee table in the living room, just beginning to work on a puzzle made from a photo of a rainforest—deep-green trees beneath a cerulean sky awash in bright sunshine. The picture was gorgeous, and putting the puzzle together was a meditation on natural beauty—one of several reasons Dora loved puzzles made from images of nature.

Missy had just begun a difficult *sudoku* and was running through the twenty or so solutions she used as a foundation for solving the puzzles.

Comfort lay with his chin on one of Freedom's brown haunches, his eyes half open, the sun from the living room windows warming the backs of both dogs. One of Comfort's ears was turned inside out. Freedom was snoring and occasionally rearranging her legs, taking care not to dislodge Comfort.

"Where do we go from here?" Dora asked.

"Are you asking about our day together or about the case?" Missy responded, teasing.

"The case, silly. We've got little bits of information, but no big picture tying them together."

"You know how this has gone in the past," Missy encouraged. "We keep working, digging, talking to people, researching. The results will come. The big picture will come into focus."

"Right." Dora went back to her puzzle.

"What's wrong?" Missy asked.

"Nothing."

"Really?"

"Really."

Missy watched Dora work her puzzle. "Why don't we call Sarah," she said. "She'll give us a fresh perspective—the point of view of the press."

"Nah."

"What does *that* mean?"

Dora looked up and stared at Missy for a moment. "It's a colloquial expression—kind of a relaxed way of saying no."

"Well, now I know you're pissed."

"Not at you."

"At Sarah."

Dora sighed. "I just don't want to see her."

Missy waited.

"We should have been invited to that fuckin' party! She was part of that—of the party being arranged. Christine and Charlie should have invited us, and Sarah should have made sure of it. These people say they're our friends."

"Dora. Look at me."

Dora looked up.

"They *are* our friends, and you're being petty."

"Am I?"

Neither Dora nor Missy spoke for a moment, then Dora got up and went into the bedroom. A few minutes later, she emerged, gym bag in hand.

"Going to work out."

"Dor, come on! Talk to me."

"Later."

• • •

Fifteen minutes later, she was at Shay's Mixed Martial Arts. No one was there but Shay, who was sweeping the dojo.

"Work out?" Dora asked.

Shay grinned, her dark eyes smiling, and asked, "Okay to hug?"

Dora returned her smile, and the two women hugged.

Shay was several inches shorter than Dora, with long black hair in a single braid that was anchored beneath one of the shoulder straps of her singlet so she could spar with little chance of her hair being pulled.

Once Dora had changed into sweats, she returned to the workout room and began stretching, after which she ran through several of her most challenging forms and practiced her repertoire of strikes, elbows, knees, and kicks. They then went over clinch work and transitioning via various techniques, from standing to the ground.

They then donned pads and headgear and agreed to spar for three two-minute rounds.

Shay set the timer, and the two women began circling one another.

Dora kicked at the back of Shay's lead leg once, then twice.

Shay jabbed and circled, darting in close, then sliding out and away —utilizing angles.

Dora slid inside and jabbed, followed by a straight right and a left hook. All but the hook connected.

Shay changed levels and took Dora to the ground, where Dora sought submissions—first a guillotine, then an arm bar.

The round ended.

When the next round began, Dora attempted a head kick, which Shay blocked. Then she dove for Dora's legs, securing the takedown. As Dora scrambled for a submission, Shay pressed herself close to Dora, smothering her attempts.

Dora decided to hang back and use her superior strength and size to strike at Shay, a strategy that had worked for her in the past, but Shay closed the distance and clinched, again holding Dora close and using her proximity to blunt Dora's power punches, elbows, and kicks.

Dora countered with a double-leg takedown, which Shay stuffed at first but which Dora eventually secured, lifting Shay into the air and flipping her onto the mat.

"Nice," Shay said.

Dora didn't answer. She suspected the studio owner's comment was a distracting tactic. Instead, she went for a leg lock but again found herself reversed and smothered against Shay's body, in a triangle choke, which left no room for movement.

Dora tapped. "Whoa," she said. "Where'd you learn that."

Shay grinned. "Been working on it. Sambo wrestling, different influences. Can't let a superior striker or an elite jiujitsu fighter get to you. This kind of smothering wrestling can negate both."

Dora's eyes gleamed with admiration as the two martial artists bowed to one another and embraced.

• • •

A half-hour, later Dora was home, being effusively greeted by two exuberant dogs, who fell all over each other trying to jump on her, lick her, and, of course, be given treats.

Missy was at the dining room table, her laptop and a mug of coffee in front of her.

Dora went to her, circled her arms around Missy's neck, and kissed her. "Sorry," she said.

"Feeling better?"

Dora nodded. "Nothing like a good ass-whuppin' to lift your spirits. But I guess I would take a different approach than Christine and Charlie if we were having a party, you know? To each their own, I guess."

Missy looked at her. "There are any number of reasons we weren't invited to Livvie's first birthday party. None of which means they don't like us."

"Let's send a gift." Dora pulled up a chair next to Missy. "Pull up Amazon, and we'll find something for a one-year-old who has Down syndrome."

Missy turned to Dora. "Is your phone on?"

Dora got up and went to the couch, then pulled her phone from her gym bag. "Nope."

"Figured. Thelma called. Maverick Lockhart wants us to call him."

"Let's call him now."

Missy agreed. Dora dialed and set the phone to speaker.

"Dora Ellison for Maverick Lockhart," Dora said to the woman who answered.

After a moment, Maverick's voice said, "Thanks for getting back to me. What have you got?"

Dora ran through their case notes.

"In other words, you've got nothing." He sounded disappointed.

"What we have," Dora corrected, "is a case in progress."

Maverick was silent. "Well, I've talked to the police, and from what I can tell, they're standing around, wringing their hands. They've got nothing. No clues. No information. They're shutting me out."

"I can assure you, Mr. Lockhart," Missy interjected, "we're not do-ing that."

"I didn't say you were."

"We're on this, sir. Nose to grindstone. But these things take a while."

"Okay," he said reluctantly. "But let's try to move it along. After even a few days, a murder case tends to go cold and is harder to work, from what I know."

"We're on it, Mr. Lockhart," Dora assured him again. "Back to you soon."

Dora put her phone down on the table. "Man watches too many cop shows."

Missy gave a wry smile. "Or reads too many mysteries."

• • •

Ganderson took one of the two sandwiches from the bag that had just been delivered from the local deli. "Tuna, lettuce, tomato, and Swiss—mine." He took a can of Diet Coke and a napkin, then returned to his desk.

Mallard took the remaining sandwich, which was turkey breast and provolone with tomato and mustard. He opened several napkins, made them into a tablecloth, and lay his still wrapped sandwich on top. He opened the other soda, which was Dr. Pepper, and sat down at his desk, looking across at Ganderson. "We need to focus on motive. We have no motive."

"We do have a very specific sort of bullet."

Mallard took a bite of his sandwich and sat back. It was delicious. "Yeah, well. Where does that get us?"

Ganderson took big bites of his sandwich, leaving a faint ring of mayonnaise around his mouth, which he wiped away with his napkin. "We have Maverick Lockhart's accountant, if that's what she is, doing shady tricks with money while also working at the Montgomery School."

They ate for a while in silence amidst the midday tumult of the busy police precinct.

"I'll tell you what," Ganderson said.

"What?"

"We need to take a deeper look into Maverick Lockhart's businesses. If the accountant, Rabelson, was shady … Where there's smoke, you know? So maybe someone wanted to get at him by going after his son."

Mallard took the last bite of his sandwich, chewed, and swallowed, washing it down with Dr. Pepper. "Agreed."

Chapter 13

Dora, Missy, and Adam Geller were at their respective desks in the back of Geller Investigations. Adam was sharing his latest tale of medical woe with Dora while Missy perused the Montgomery School's website for possible clues.

Adam had slid a portable ice pack down into the side of his pants, which held it close against his hip.

"I'm in so much pain from thirty years of arthritis that I get into bed, and it's just such a relief! And then, the curse is I have to pee literally every forty-five seconds, so I've gotta get up!" He shook his head, exhaustion plain on his face, along with a hint of a twinkle in his eye, as though he was devastated but somehow able to drum up a modicum of humor about his situation.

Dora thought that remarkable, if a little too much information. "Sorry, Adam. That's gotta suck," she said.

He snorted, scoffing. "Don't get old, young lady."

"What's the alternative?"

"Going out with a blaze of glory?"

Dora thought it was interesting that when he focused on the conversation at hand, when he was engaged, the pain vanished from his face.

"Dor, c'mere." Missy was staring with interest at something on her screen. Dora pushed off with her feet and rolled her chair until she was next to Missy. She looked at the screen. On it was the biography of an associate dean at the Montgomery School.

"This guy, Crayton Warbler," Missy said, "seems to be actively involved in school security and near the top of the food chain at Montgomery. I'm wondering if we should talk to him, pick his brain about what went on, how it could have happened, and so forth. Maybe he has insight into conflicts within the school or between the school and its community."

"Excellent," Dora said. "Do you want to call Montgomery and set up an appointment?"

"On it." Missy navigated to the contact page and, seeing no direct line for Warbler, called the main office. "This is Missy Winters with Geller Investigations. We're looking into Julian Lockhart's murder. I'd like to set up an appointment with Crayton Warbler."

"Mr. Warbler is very busy," the woman in the main office said. "You'll have to call back in a few days."

"Well, if he's busy, why don't we just make an appointment to see him whenever he's available."

"That won't be possible. He's made clear that—"

"This is a murder investigation," Missy insisted.

"Are you with the police?"

"No, we're a private—"

"Please call back in a few days."

The line went dead.

Missy turned to Dora. "Did you hear that?"

"Not really."

"I can't even make an appointment to see this guy. They say I have to call back in a few days."

Dora considered this. "Let's call Gloria Steinmetz and maybe Fred Chase. Maybe they'll be able to tell us something about this Warbler guy. Give us the lay of the land. Then, if we need to, we can call the principal."

Missy dialed.

"Put it on speaker, please," Dora said.

"Gloria Steinmetz? This is Missy Winters at Geller Investigations. How are you? How's Penny?"

"As long as the music's playing, she's okay. But when her thoughts wander to Julian, she tends to get upset, and she can get caught in a sort of loop of logic, where her upset builds on itself and— But you don't need to hear my troubles. How can I help?"

Missy said, "We were wondering what you could tell us about someone who works at Montgomery. A dean? Name of Warbler?"

"Oh, Mr. Warbler. Penny is terrified of him. Quite a few of them are."

"Really? Why?"

"I don't know. He's never done anything wrong, as far as I can tell, but Penny and some of the others think he's evil."

"Evil?"

Gloria Steinmetz sighed. "The only information I've been able to get out of her is that he's creepy and evil."

Missy looked at Dora, eyebrows arched. "But he hasn't hurt anyone as far as you know?"

"That's correct, as far as I know. But the perception goes beyond Penny. I've spoken to some of the other parents and family members via Facebook chats. There's a common perception that he's an evil man."

• • •

At seven thirty, Ganderson and Mallard pulled up in front of a single-story Cape Cod with cedar shake siding and flowers growing in a curved dirt-and-mulch bed that was neatly cut into the lawn in front of the house.

Mallard was doing his best to get off the phone. "Look, Kay. It's none of our business what they did with their hedges. Their hedges are their business." He rolled his eyes at Ganderson. "So, if they stepped onto our property when they were cutting them, I'll have a talk with them and ask them to cut only their side of the hedges. Listen, I have to go, Kay. Let's pick this up—" He held his phone away from his face. "She hung up."

"Well, that right there is why—" Ganderson began.

"No need to expound on the virtues of a single life. I've had enough arguing for one day."

"Suit yourself." Ganderson got out of the car, and Mallard followed. They approached the door of the blue house; a white Ford Escape was parked in the driveway. Mallard rang the bell.

The woman who answered the door was heavyset, with beige skin, tired, lined eyes, a broad nose, and medium-brown hair that was pulled back and held in place with a plastic barrette. "Yes?" she said.

Ganderson held up a badge. The woman waited.

"Virginia Rabelson? Ganderson said.

"Yes."

"Might be better if we came in," Mallard said.

She stood aside and ushered the detectives into a rather messy living room. A sweater lay on the couch, another on the back of a chair. Several empty popcorn bags were on a coffee table in front of a green suede couch.

"Sorry about the mess. Wasn't expecting company." She sat down on the couch and nodded for them to sit. "You're here about the Montgomery School. What would you like to know?"

"Actually," Mallard said, "we're here to learn more about your relationship with the victim's father, Maverick Lockhart."

The woman looked startled. "I don't know what you mean."

"Sure you do," Ganderson said, smiling.

Mallard could see his partner was itching for a conflict. "You're an accountant, am I right?" Mallard asked.

"That's right," Rabelson said, nodding. "I work for the Montgomery School, in the business office."

"But you work for Maverick Lockhart on the side."

"I work for several local businesses," she corrected. "Two restaurants, a laundromat, three bars, and a store that sells CBD products."

"The thing that ties these places together, other than the fact that you work for them," Mallard said, his tone growing more forceful, "is that Maverick Lockhart owns a stake in each of them. Are we correct?"

Rabelson tried to look confused. "If you say so."

"We know so," Ganderson said, staring at her, unblinking.

Rabelson shrugged. Mallard could see the fear behind her wall of feigned ignorance.

"So," he said. "To clarify. You're maintaining that you work for these mom-and-pop businesses …"

"I handle their accounting, yes. I'm a private contractor."

"And you claim to have no knowledge of Maverick Lockhart's involvement with each of them?"

Again the fear in her eyes. She forced a nod.

Ganderson held out his pad and pen. "Would you write down the names of the businesses you work for and whomever you deal with at each one?"

• • •

"Let's call the principal." Dora pulled out her phone, performed a Google search, and pressed the number.

"I'd like to make an appointment to see Principal Sumner, please," she said into the phone. She widened her eyes at Missy as if to say, "This is a good idea."

Turning her attention back to the phone, she said, "Tell her it's Dora Ellison, from Geller Investigations. We're investigating the Lockhart murder. I'll be with Missy Winters, of the same company." She covered the phone with her hand and looked at Missy. "This should get us into the building." She listened again, briefly. "Sure. Two tomorrow is just fine."

Missy nodded in agreement.

The following day at one forty, Dora and Missy climbed into Dora's turbo and drove to the Montgomery School, parked, entered the building through the front entrance, and explained to the security guard that they had an appointment with Principal Sumner.

The guard looked at his list and directed them to the appropriate office. On their way, the two investigators stopped a young woman headed in the opposite direction. "Could you tell us where Dean Warbler's office is?"

The woman pointed. "Go to the end of the hallway, take the stairs to the second floor, then make a right. It's the second or third office on the left. His name's on the door."

They were several minutes early, so Dora and Missy headed to the end of the hallway, went up the stairs, and followed the instructions they'd been given until they found themselves at Dean Crayton Warbler's door.

Dora knocked.

There was no answer.

She tried the knob. It was locked.

"Let's go see Sumner, then come back," Dora suggested.

"What do we say to Sumner?" Missy asked.

Dora just smiled.

Claire Sumner rose from behind her desk when the two women entered her office. "Can I get you ladies coffee?"

Missy looked hopefully at Dora, but the latter shook her head, and said, "No thanks. We just wanted to offer you an update as to how the case is progressing."

Sumner smiled appreciatively. "That's thoughtful. Thank you."

Dora then offered a redacted version of their notes to date, leaving out certain clues and suspicions so that the information sounded substantive yet was innocuous enough not to undermine any ongoing avenues of investigation.

When they were finished, Principal Sumner thanked them and suggested they return once they had anything further to report or if they had any questions that fell under her purview.

The two women then returned to the second floor and knocked on Warbler's door.

"Come!" a voice ordered from within.

They entered and found themselves in a musty office that was spartan except for a small desk and chair in the far corner. On the chair at the desk, bent over some papers, was a small balding man with a fringe of graying dark hair, a bony nose, and intense brown eyes behind gray wire glasses. He was dressed in a jacket and slacks, a white shirt, and a gray bowtie. "Can I help you?"

Dora nodded and held out a hand. "My name is Dora Ellison, and this is Missy Winters. We're with Geller Investigations, and we're investigating the murder of Julian Lockhart."

The man's expression didn't change. Eventually, he said, "I see," but he remained hunched over the papers on his desk. "Well?" he said, finally.

"We understand that you're responsible for the security at Montgomery," Dora began.

"We were wondering whether you could shed light on how security is handled there," Missy said. "And how whoever was responsible for Julian Lockhart's death was able to gain access to the assembly with a weapon."

Warbler frowned. He sat upright and turned toward them, his shoulders bunched up around his ears. His frown was hard under his dark, hairy brow and had the malevolence of a glare.

"I take pride in my work here. I make certain that the systems required to run an institution for special people—people who have many different special needs—function smoothly and correctly." He stood up so suddenly that both Dora and Missy stepped back.

"Are you suggesting that I'm somehow responsible for that horror last week?" The man's glare had withered into a sneer.

"We're not suggesting anything at all," Dora answered. "We came to gather information. To learn, not to suggest or accuse."

"Well," Warbler said, a corner of his upper lip curling. "I suggest you ask whatever you came to ask, and leave me to my work!"

"We came to ask your opinion," Dora said in an attempt to lower the temperature of the conversation.

He gave a mirthless laugh. "My opinion is that as far as I'm concerned, I did my job. What else would I know about someone murdering one of our people?"

"That's what we came to ask you," Dora calmly replied.

"Enough!" He pounded his fist on his desk, sat down, and made a shooing motion several times with his left hand. "Time for you to leave!"

Chapter 14

Sarah sat on a stool at the bar that divided her kitchen from her living room. She had Livvie pressed against a small blanket that covered her shoulder. She patted her daughter's back while arguing with LaChance, who was seated on her living room sofa.

"How is it our place to run an editorial demanding Claire Sumner's removal?" Sarah demanded to know.

LaChance wore a pressed checkered shirt and brown slacks with a leather belt. He smiled while thoughtfully stroking his goatee. "If we're the voice of the people, doesn't it follow that we're also the conscience of the people?"

Livvie let out a throaty burp and spit up on the blanket, which Sarah was grateful was large enough to cover her entire shoulder, including her back—Livvie's frequent target area. "Sure, but Montgomery is a specialized school. We don't know what we don't know, so casting blame would be irresponsible, don't you think?"

To Sarah, LaChance was maddeningly calm. Still smiling, he said, "But we do know what we do know. There was a murder at this school —a school that cares for some of our most vulnerable citizens. Where does the buck stop?"

"The buck stops with whoever killed Julian Lockhart!" she retorted, though she had to concede that LaChance had a point. "I'm just not comfortable running an editorial demanding that the principal be fired. We're not that kind of paper."

"You brought me here to help *The Chronicle* out of a financial hole," LaChance explained, his gray almond-shaped eyes retaining a hint of humor while his mouth was set in a more stubborn line. "Taking more active positions will help us attract readers and keep them engaged, which will help ad sales. It's a cycle, but not a vicious one."

"Well," Sarah replied, "that sounds nice, but really, what experience do you have running a newspaper?"

"What experience do you have running a financially successful business?" He looked down, then up again with a chastened expression. "Look, I'm sorry. I don't mean to be confrontational. These are recommendations, but I'm putting up my own money to support *The Chronicle*. I hope you'll consider my suggestions as intended to be helpful to our paper's financial well-being."

Sarah said nothing, though she didn't like the reference to "*our* paper," despite there being truth to it.

As soon as LaChance was gone, Sarah wiped Livvie's mouth with an edge of the blanket a second time, then went to a hamper in the kitchen and dropped the blanket in. She walked to a small pile of clean blankets on the kitchen counter, took one, and laid it over her shoulder. Livvie laid her head down and was instantly asleep.

Sarah looked at her phone and saw C3's text. He was going to an NA meeting after work and wouldn't be home until nine thirty.

She put Livvie in her car seat, which had a mechanized rocker attachment that helped her sleep. But Livvie was now wide awake, so Sarah said to Livvie what she'd planned to say to C3. "Isn't LaChance here to help? Shouldn't he be a net positive?"

Livvie looked back at Sarah and blinked several times. Perhaps it was better that she talked to Livvie than C3 about her issues with LaChance; C3's recovery was sacrosanct. These issues with LaChance might be dangerous territory for C3, who needed his sponsor on his side 100 percent of the time.

"Where does he get off trying to dictate editorial policy? I mean, isn't it a little arrogant for us to advocate for the firing of an official at a special school?"

Livvie watched her mother closely, absorbing the nuances of her facial expression and feeling her own nameless emotions.

• • •

As soon as Ganderson showed him a badge, the demeanor of Sajan Khatri, the Lucky Card and Vape Shop's owner, morphed from suspicious to gracious.

"I'm always happy to talk to the police!" he exclaimed, then said something unintelligible to the boy who was helping at the counter. He beckoned the detectives to the back of the store. Mallard had the impression that while Khatri might have been open to talking to the police, he was less open to being seen doing so.

Khatri bid Ganderson and Mallard sit on the only two chairs in the back room, which was a riot of open boxes of vape-related products, cheap children's toys, tea bags, candy, cigarette cartons, and gift cards.

"Don't you want to sit?" Mallard asked.

"No, no! I sit all day behind the counter! Please." He plugged in a small portable teapot, took three tea bags from an open box, and deposited them in mugs that were crowded onto a round table. "Please join me for some blue tea."

"Blue tea?" asked Ganderson.

"Very good for stress and skin." Khatri peered at Ganderson, and, in response, the detective self-consciously rubbed his pockmarked face and frowned.

The teapot had been recently used, and the water was ready within less than a minute. Khatri poured, and the detectives watched as the water in the mugs turned blue.

"Look at that," Mallard marveled.

"Huh. Blue tea," Ganderson said.

"How can I help?" Khatri asked.

"Do you know a Maverick Lockhart?" Ganderson asked.

Khatri's expression didn't change; he appeared to think deeply. "I—I'm not sure. The name is familiar."

"We're asking," Mallard said, "because we know him to be your business partner." He looked steadily at the store owner. "It'd be a shame if we were to find out you were lying to us."

"Ah yes—Maverick Lockhart!" Khatri smiled and looked surprised at his own suddenly refreshed memory.

"What can you tell us about him?" Ganderson queried.

"Nothing much," Khatri responded, dipping his tea bag obsessively into the water in his mug. The detectives didn't touch their tea. "Please," Khatri encouraged, "drink."

The detectives lifted their mugs from the table, but still, neither drank.

"Maverick Lockhart," Ganderson pressed.

Khatri shrugged. "He's a businessman. He helps small businesses like mine."

"In exchange for … " Mallard prodded.

"A small percentage of my business. What else?" the store owner said, his tone implying that the detectives should have known this.

Mallard said, "You know he recently lost his son."

Khatri shook his head sadly. "A terrible thing. Terrible thing. The absolute worst."

"What happens if you don't pay Lockhart?" Mallard asked.

"We have an agreement. My part is I pay, and I do. I always do. Mr. Lockhart is never a problem for me, and I'm never a problem for him. Never."

Khatri seemed to have nothing to add, so the detectives moved on to the next name on their list—Sunfield Gas Station and Auto Repair, owned by Tomasino Giardelli.

At the gas station, the detectives wandered into a small empty office that sold energy drinks, snacks, candy, gum, beef jerky, and cigarettes as well as gas. Outside, a bearded attendant, who had long black sideburns and was wearing a denim vest over a white T-shirt and dirty black pants, was pumping gas.

"Hello?" Ganderson called toward the repair area, which was through a side doorway.

"Yo!" a voice called. "In here."

The detectives walked into the repair area, which consisted of two bays behind open garage doors. In one bay was a maroon 2018 Impala, which was up on a lift, and in the other was a 2014 Honda Accord with its hood up. The bays appeared to be empty of people.

"Hello?" Ganderson called again.

"Right here!" came the answer.

Giardelli slid out from beneath the Honda; he was olive-skinned and clean-shaven, with dark eyebrows, dyed black hair, a receding hairline, and a widow's peak. He was in his mid-forties, perhaps fifteen pounds overweight, and he wore a pair of dirty coveralls over a green shirt. On the left breast of the coveralls was a white cloth patch with a red embroidered border and script lettering that read "The Boss."

Ganderson flashed his badge. Giardelli led them back to the office and sat behind the desk. The two detectives took seats opposite him.

"You do business with a Maverick Lockhart?" Ganderson asked.

Giardelli looked from one detective to the other. "What's this about?"

"Do you?" Mallard asked.

Giardelli shrugged. "What if I do? I haven't done anything wrong."

"Did we say you did?" Ganderson stared at Giardelli.

"So?"

"What can you tell us about him?"

Giardelli shrugged and looked away. "He's a guy who helps small businesses in the area. He helped me. Got nothing bad to say about him."

"How?" Mallard asked.

"Loaned me money."

"Like a vig?" Ganderson quickly asked.

"He loaned me money," Giardelli repeated and shrugged.

Ganderson got up and began walking around the office, peering at products that were for sale; he then wandered into the repair bays. When he returned, he said, "Looks to me like you've got a bunch of violations. A bunch," he emphasized.

"Fuck. What do you want?" Giardelli asked, looking directly at Ganderson.

"Information."

"Like?"

"How Lockhart operates."

"He loans people money."

"More information than that," Mallard pressed.

Giardelli sighed. "He finds out who's in financial trouble and loans them money for a cut going forward. Then he encourages them to borrow more to grow the business, or for protection."

"Protection from what," Ganderson asked.

"From him."

Ganderson nodded.

"Eventually," Giardelli continued, "at least with some people, he owns most of the business."

"We know," Mallard said.

"So what happens when you don't pay, or you pay late, or you pay too little?" Ganderson asked.

"Well, first he makes sure you know it."

"How?"

"He tells you," said Giardelli. "He just tells you. Says not to do it. Don't pay late. The message is clear. You have to know the guy. You just know to not do it. It's clear in his tone."

Mallard glanced at Ganderson, then back at Giardelli. "And what if you still fall short or don't pay?"

"Then he sends someone. Then you pay."

Chapter 15

The Goose and the Gander were seated at a corner table in a Starbucks, each sipping their coffee. They'd chosen the table because it was away from both the aisles most of the customers walked along and the windows. The location had the dual benefit of keeping their profile low and the midday sun out of their eyes.

"Why do you drink that treacly crap?" Ganderson chinned toward Mallard's frothy cup, which was filled with his beloved mixture of iced coffee, chocolate syrup, sweetener, half-and-half, and whipped cream.

"What kind of word is *treacly*?" Mallard retorted. "What's it from— *Alice in Wonderland*?"

Mallard's phone buzzed. He looked at it. "Your girlfriend," he said, grinning at his partner, who looked away. "Mallard," he said into the phone. He listened, said, "Thanks, Cathy," and then ended the call.

"Now, this is interesting." He stood up. "Come on." Still annoyed by Ganderson's comment about his treacly drink, he made a point of not explaining Lieutenant Trask's reason for calling.

Ganderson had no choice but to follow.

Several minutes later, they pulled up in front of Jack Ashford's bayfront home. A loud cracking sound was coming from the backyard. Mallard led the way around the side of the house, reached over to open a side gate, and proceeded into the yard.

Jack Ashford was standing on one side of his half-acre yard, aiming a rifle at twin paper targets that hung from a metal stand. The targets were white with concentric red circles expanding from the centers and rectangles near the corners.

Ganderson looked reproachfully at Mallard, who grinned, delighted to have important knowledge his partner lacked. Their relationship was an endless passive-aggressive pissing contest, which both men relished but neither would admit to.

"Mr. Ashford!" Mallard called.

Ashford turned, leaned the rifle against a chair, and approached the detectives with a hand out. Neither shook it.

"What you're doing is against the law," Mallard stated, looking from Ashford to the rifle and back again.

"I'm on my property," Ashford protested. "And there's no chance of my hitting anything or anyone out on the water."

"Ricochets are always possible," Ganderson countered.

"There's a playground on the water not far from here." Mallard gave Ashford what he thought of as his cop stare. He liked to say it could wither flowers in springtime.

Ashford looked crestfallen. "Well, I know that. But how far is it? How far does it have to be, by law?"

"Five hundred feet," Mallard said with assurance.

Ashford held up a hand. "I apologize, Officers."

"Detectives," Ganderson corrected.

"Detectives. My bad."

"Got that right," Mallard said.

"That's a marksman's rifle, isn't it?" Ganderson asked, with a glance at Mallard.

"Well, yes. I enjoy shooting for accuracy," Ashford said, shading his eyes from the sun with a palm.

"What kind of rounds you got there?" Ganderson continued, squinting at Ashford.

Ashford paused. "It's a .300 Win Mag."

Ganderson took out his notebook and thumbed through it, then asked. "Will your rifle shoot a .338 Lapua Magnum?"

Ashford's lower lip curled outward. "Don't know. Why?"

"That's the round that was pulled out of the padding at the back of the stage after your grandson was killed." Ganderson was looking hard at Ashford, who took off his glasses and stared right back.

"Maybe you oughta have another look at your little notebook there, because I was in the audience when my boy was killed. I was the first person up on that stage with his head in my arms, where he passed. I didn't happen to have a rifle with me. And I resent the implication."

"There was no implication," Mallard said.

Ashford didn't blink, but Ganderson did. "Just see to it that you don't do any more target shooting out here," he said.

• • •

"Well, I don't see any accidents." Missy was walking around the apartment, followed by Comfort, who was still prancing at her heels, overjoyed that Dora and Missy were home. Freedom waited in the kitchen for her customary snack. She'd jumped up and licked Dora's face, done the same to Missy, then trotted into the kitchen as a not-so-subtle hint.

"And the kids seem okay," Dora said.

They'd tentatively agreed to hire Wayne, a short orange-haired man with small sharp eyes, to walk the dogs during the day and feed them in the afternoon. Business at Geller Investigations had grown to the point where both women were needed nearly full-time every day, and Adam's participation was significantly less than it had been—both qualitatively and quantitatively. Their boss was now on crutches full-time, awaiting a hip replacement, and had to be near a bathroom, given the side effects of his cancer radiation treatments.

Dora opened Freedom's bag of snacks, and the rottweiler-Doberman mix began barking in anticipation.

"What d'ya say, kids? Are we going with Wayne?" Missy had returned to the kitchen, where Comfort saw that his best friend was eating, so he loudly demanded equal compensation.

Dora gave Missy an encouraging but questioning look. "His refs look good, and if the app says it's okay …"

"I'll text him through the app. He said he could start tomorrow if we approve."

"Well," Dora said, "then I approve. Big load off our shoulders."

"Yup," Missy replied. "What do you want to do about Warbler?"

Dora took a beer from the fridge, sat down at the dining room table, and cracked it open. "I could see how Penny Bright thinks he's scary. He's weird."

"And she's so cheerful," Missy ventured. "He's like a dark cloud on her sunny day."

"I love when you're poetic."

Missy had opened her laptop and was suddenly engaged with something. After a moment, she slid the computer toward Dora for her to see the screen. "Got his address."

Dora was impressed.

"Easy enough. Let's go and lean on him," Missy suggested.

"And say what?" Dora wanted to know.

"You'll think of something on the way."

Dora grinned. "You're right. Great minds …"

Twelve minutes later, they pulled up in front of a red brick house with twin second-floor windows that stared out at the street like eyes, their window shades like half-lowered lids. The front of the house was nearly hidden by vines that crawled up the brick and extended green and brown tentacles onto the roof, adding a beard to the face metaphor.

Dora rang the bell, which chimed inside the house.

The door was answered by a tiny woman with close-cropped gray hair, painted-on brown eyebrows, and crimson lipstick.

"Are you running for office?" she wanted to know.

Dora laughed. "Hardly!"

"I thought I recognized you from the newspaper."

"Possibly, but that would have been some time ago," Missy explained.

"Is Mr. Warbler in?" Dora asked.

"My son is upstairs, I think," the woman said.

"Your son?" Dora mused.

"You wanted Crayton, you said, yes?"

Dora nodded, and the woman disappeared.

"Her son?" Dora marveled. Crayton Warbler looked to her to be at least as old as the woman who'd answered the door.

Several minutes later, Crayton Warbler returned to the door alone, looking more like a chastened little boy than a villainous old man. His sheepish expression changed to one of alarm when he saw Dora and Missy. He opened the screen door several inches. "You can't be here!" he complained.

"So invite us in!" Dora replied.

Warbler looked at them from beneath veiled eyelids, then sighed and held the door slightly farther ajar, allowing the two investigators into his home. He took a single step back, allowing Dora and Missy to take only one step into the dark living room. An elongated Modigliani woman stared at them from a painting on a wall beyond the doorway. Dora knew nothing about Modigliani except that Missy hated the man's work. She found his paintings to be creepy—their faces otherworldly and vaguely appalling. From beyond the painting, through a narrow doorway, War-bler's mother watched, as silent as the Modigliani on the wall.

"Well?" he demanded, and Dora could feel some strong emotion ra-diating from the man. But the emotion wasn't frightening or nefarious; it was a sense of boxed-in paranoia—a particular brand of fear.

"I don't know what it is you're trying to do by hounding me like this, but my job is important to me. I need my job—to support myself and my mother. Whatever this is about, whatever you need, let's get it over with, and then please get out of my life!"

"Okay," Dora said.

That Warbler was frightened left him in a position to be questioned, yet perhaps driven toward dishonesty and deception for the sake of self-preservation.

"Isn't it true that you dislike Mason Montgomery?" Dora asked.

Warbler looked surprised. "Dislike?" He raised an eyebrow thoughtfully. "The buck stops with him, doesn't it? He puts pressure on me. It's part of my being a dean." He leaned toward Dora and Missy. "But what I can't stand about him is that he's not going to keep the place going." His tone changed from conspiratorial to aggressive indignation. "He could, you know! He could set up a trust. The man has nearly $2 billion and a son who needs this place."

"But his son doesn't come to Montgomery," Missy protested.

Warbler gave her a withering look. "All the more reason for him to upgrade. He could build the facility around his son's needs. I'm pretty sure that's what he did originally—only his son's condition grew more serious. And we have other wings. He might very well do just fine in another area of the facility." He paused. "You're right. I dislike Mason Montgomery. But did I try to kill him and accidentally kill Julian Lockhart? Come on!"

• • •

"What do you think?" Dora asked, when they were back in the car.

Missy looked thoughtful. "I think he's a man who needs to keep his job. To paraphrase: did he try to kill Montgomery and maybe miss and kill Julian Lockhart? I don't know. I doubt it."

"Weird little man," Dora commented. "Can you call Claire Sumner and Robert or Sean, or one of the aides who oversee the people at Montgomery? Maybe we talk to one of the aides next—find out if Warbler was at the assembly."

"Right—maybe Kelvin. He watches Vanessa Burrell's sons."

Dora looked surprised. "How do you know that?"

Missy gave a sheepish shrug. "Facebook."

An hour later they had their answer. Neither Kelvin nor Sean remembered seeing Warbler at the assembly at which Julian Lockhart was killed. Claire Sumner said she remembered that Crayton Warbler had called in sick that morning, then asked whether that fact was relevant to the case. Missy, who'd made the calls as she and Dora were driving home, didn't answer that question.

Chapter 16

Lonny finished shaving his head, noted the spots that were bleeding, and tore off bits of toilet paper, which he stuck to the blood. While having a cigarette, he'd decided to go the firing range, something he'd first decided against, but the lure of shooting—the release it brought—was too strong. After having a cigarette, he removed the bits of paper, washed off the remaining spots of blood, checked the cash in his wallet, and headed for the truck.

He was relieved that Tommy Bannion had agreed to let him keep his Ruger at the range. Driving with her in the cab, or even hidden in the truck bed, would have weighed on his mind, and walking to and from the car with a rifle case would have been just as stressful.

He felt good about going to the range. Doing something he was so good at—target shooting—left him feeling happily empty—discharged. As though he'd just fucked someone. Release and relief.

He'd thought that the relief from being out from under the vig would be greater, but he had no way of earning anywhere near enough money to keep his apartment and the truck and had no idea where to look. Work in a supermarket? A gas station? He wouldn't have known how to find much else. And then he knew: delivering cocaine. And he'd known just where to ask.

The problem was that delivering cocaine led to using cocaine—or at least badly wanting to. So now he was delivering and spending just under half the money he earned on his habit. He had to admit he had a blow habit.

He shot pool in the early afternoons at the BS Pool Hall in the west end, and he delivered blow in the evening, when the rich assholes were home—rich assholes being anyone with an income greater than about $50,000.

No longer did he owe; no longer could muscle show up and work him over because he owed. He was free of that, which was an enormous weight off his shoulders. He was vig- and debt-free, so he was trying to decide what to do with the rest of his life. Was there a woman he could get involved with? A motorcycle to buy? The problem was, his true affairs were with shooting and blow—and both were expensive.

• • •

Dora and Missy were lying in bed, facing in opposite directions. Each had two pillows beneath her head and was looking at her own iPad, reading shared case notes on a Google Drive.

Dora spoke first, scrolling the document with her left index finger. "This situation with Jack Ashford is just plain weird. It makes sense for him to hate Mason Montgomery because that's who he believes put his grandson at risk by going back on what we're told was his word—by not keeping the school open."

"Well," said Missy, still looking at her iPad. "A lot of people are angry with Montgomery." She watched Comfort, who leaped up on the bed and pushed his paw against Missy's iPad, forcing it away from her field of vision. She raised the iPad again, and Comfort again swiped it away. Missy laughed. "Check it out. Comfort won't let me use my iPad!"

"Well, you should be playing with him. That's why you exist," Dora said. "Or didn't you know?"

"Yeah, well. Comfort, I need to work!" Missy stroked the top of his head with her palm. She slid her fingers over the area between his eyes, which fluttered closed in ecstasy. "No, no," she said gently. "I need to work." She lifted him back to the floor and resumed reading from her screen. "In one sense, Jack Ashford has more motive than anyone else—at least if we're looking at Montgomery being the target."

"Because he's older than most of the parents?" Dora asked.

"Well, yeah. Because his grandson would need help sooner—at a younger age—without a guardian."

"That makes sense," Dora said. "As far as it goes. But that he would try to kill Montgomery … I don't know about that."

"I know," Missy insisted. "Even assuming he was driven by enough fear and rage. But what really doesn't make sense would be trying to do it and accidentally killing your own grandson."

"You know what?" Dora mused. "It does make sense, of a sort."

"What sort?" Missy asked.

"Karmic sense."

"I suppose," Missy offered, "we could theorize that he killed his grandson on purpose so the young man wouldn't lack for care once he, Ashford, was gone."

Dora thought about this. "It makes logical sense. But it's just crazy."

"Well, okay," Missy began. "So, how do we unravel Jack Ashford?"

Dora was silent, then brightened. "I have an idea."

• • •

There were three shooting ranges within an hour's drive from Beach City. The detectives had been in touch with all three, requesting that they keep tabs on handgun and rifle models—and their owners—that showed up. Ganderson insisted they visit each range in person rather than call, since reading the tells of evasive people of interest would be just about impossible on the phone.

Sidney Lowenstein ran the nearest range, three towns northeast of Beach City. He was a small blocky man in his mid-sixties, with gray hair that retained a bit of brown.

"We get quite a few serious shooters, especially on Friday evenings and Saturday afternoons," Lowenstein said in a gravelly voice. He was dressed in a forest-green polo shirt and khaki shorts with high white sweat socks. He added, "But nothing that would shoot an armor-piercing AP485."

Mallard, who did most of the talking, thanked Lowenstein. He and Ganderson got back into the car and drove into Queens, where both of the remaining shooting ranges were located.

Calvin Dinwiddy ran the second range with his wife, Suzy. An obese couple in matching tactical outfits, they, too, said they hadn't seen any- one with anything that would fire the round Ganderson showed them.

The third range was run by Tom Bannion, a freckled man known lo- cally as a champion marksman. His head was perpetually cocked to the right, perhaps from a lifetime of looking through rifle sights. He was preternaturally still, his movements spare and efficient. He emitted an intensity, a feeling of focused, coiled energy.

He glanced at Ganderson, smiled slightly when shown the bullet, and gave Mallard a long look as if making a decision. "Follow me," he said, then walked through an iron door behind the counter toward the rear of the facility. The two detectives followed.

As he walked, Bannion removed a key from a crowded key ring that had jangled on his hip. Then he approached a heavy oak door that was padlocked shut and used the key to open the padlock.

Inside the room were three walls. All except the one in which the door was located were covered with gun racks filled with stacked stock-down rifles of all kinds—single-barrel, double-barrel, long-barrel, sawed-off, semiautomatic, fully automatic, legal, illegal, classic, and modern. They were crowded floor to ceiling and filled the width of the walls.

"Lot of folks don't want to keep these in the house," Bannion said.

"Why not?" Ganderson asked him, curious.

"Lots of reasons. Kids could get at 'em, someone gets depressed and uses 'em to end it. But mostly to keep them safe, and at the right temperature and humidity. My safe room is always at seventy degrees Fahrenheit and 50 percent humidity. Always."

He walked to a spot on the far wall and pointed to a long black rifle with a large scope and a muzzle brake, which was several guns from the left edge.

"This could be what you're looking for," Bannion said, with more than a hint of admiration in his voice. "Ruger Precision Gen 3 Bolt-Action—a sniper's dream. Fires your .338 Lapua Mag loaded with your armor-piercing AP485."

"Does it belong to your range?" Ganderson asked.

"Nope. Belongs to a customer—a good one."

"Who?" Ganderson wanted to know.

Bannion raised his eyebrows. "Well, I don't know about that. He's in here at least once a week. Probably drops five hunnert a month here."

"All we want is a name," Mallard said.

"I give you a name, and I may lose a good, paying customer."

"On the other hand," said Ganderson, "the local area might lose a murderer."

"Gotta make a living," Bannion insisted, shaking his head and taking a short step toward the door.

Mallard took a thick wad of cash out of his left pants pocket. He peeled off five bills and handed them to Bannion, who glanced at them and stuffed them into a pocket. "Richard Dubon, goes by Lonny." He wrote down an address and phone number on a small piece of note paper and handed it to Ganderson.

• • •

Look at this," said Missy.

"What?"

"In *The Chronicle*. A guest editorial by someone with the initials L. R. They're saying that Mason Montgomery is the cause of this violence—I guess the writer means Julian Lockhart's murder—by having all these so-called cripples and morons invading our city. Blame Montgomery and blame the mayor, the writer says." She looked at Dora with a pained expression. "How can Sarah print something like this? What kind of paper is *The Chronicle* becoming?"

"Let me see," Dora said as she brought up the current issue of *The Chronicle* on her iPad. "And the person goes on to say, 'These people have no business in Beach City, which is for "normal people" to enjoy and have fun.' That's crazy. I wonder what's up with Sarah."

• • •

LaChance was sitting at Sarah's kitchen table, listening as she read bits of emails, texts, and social media posts *The Chronicle* had received during the previous two days.

"'Allowing this kind of trash into your publication is the height of fake news bullshit,'" LaChance read. He beamed, his features animated with excitement. "Here's another one. 'About time *The Chronicle* started telling it like it is! These disabled people deserve a good home—just not here.'" He looked up at Sarah, whose elbows were on the table, one hand covering her mouth.

"What are we going to do about this?" she wanted to know. "This is crazy, and not how I run my newspaper."

"No, it's not," LaChance said. "You run your newspaper into the ground and lose your shirt. *This* is how you run a *profitable* newspaper."

She looked back at him, her voice tight, eyes narrowed. "But how am I supposed to respond editorially?"

LaChance threw up his hands. "Any way you want. It's your paper."

"Oh, *now* it's my paper," Sarah muttered. "Now that we're down to the hard decisions, it's my paper. You throw dynamite into the pile, like a pyromaniac. The shit hits the fan, and it's *my* paper."

The two stared at one another for a long moment. Then Sarah began to type, and as she typed and her words appeared on *The Chronicle*'s web feed, LaChance read aloud.

"'It is *The Chronicle*'s opinion that the students and/or attendees at the Montgomery School are entitled to the same services, protections, and inclusions as all of our residents. Yes, that includes taxpayers. The fact that you're a resident and pay taxes doesn't mean you're any better than anyone else. If anything, the special people at Montgomery need more services by virtue of their disabilities. That's what it means to live in a *civilized* society!'"

Within seconds, a comment appeared. "'Wrong! They don't pay their way—they don't deserve special services if they don't pay special taxes! People, we cannot allow this. We need to stand and fight this hijacking of what's ours by the people at the Montgomery School!'"

Sarah looked at LaChance—fear and concern in her eyes. "Look at the response! We're stirring up crazy people!"

LaChance smiled. "Know what else we're stirring up? Readers. Revenue! And, eventually, advertisers—once they see our circulation go through the roof."

Chapter 17

Dora was on the apartment floor in sweats, stretching her left hamstring by keeping her leg straight and grasping her toes. Her right leg was folded beneath her.

"Ashford's torn apart by grief," she said to Missy, "which has probably colored his judgment. It would be natural for him to blame Maverick."

"For his daughter's problems too." Missy was at the dining room table, researching on her computer.

Dora switched to her right hamstring, and, after several minutes, folded first one, then the other, leg behind her and lay back, stretching her quads. "Some people are pissed, and Ashford's one of them. Montgomery promised to keep his great school going, and now he's reneged, and they're understandably freaked out."

Comfort tore through the room, running at full speed. A moment later, Freedom loped in, following in Comfort's path. The dogs disappeared, barking, down the hallway.

Missy sat back in the dining room chair, digesting what Dora had said. "Imagine having a child with special needs—a child who really needs a lot of services—and suddenly not knowing what will become of them after you're gone because the services you planned for will no longer be there."

Dora looked at her partner. "But wouldn't those services be available elsewhere?"

"We don't know, do we? And we don't know the difference between services provided here versus somewhere else." She paused. "How do we get some perspective on Jack Ashford? How do we figure out if he's capable of murder based on that devastation or if he's a grandfather who was simply terrified for his special grandson's future?"

Dora was silent for a moment, then unfolded her legs and sat up straight. "Or if he's so twisted over this that he had his own grandson killed to spare him some unknown future. We need to get to know Ashford beyond what's available to us." She paused, then brightened. "I'll tell you how. We go see his daughter."

. . .

C3 was sitting at the dining room table with Livvie, who was in a high chair. He didn't have to go to the counseling center for another two hours, and Sarah was busy working on deadlines and other *Chronicle*-related business, so he was feeding Livvie, something he deeply enjoyed doing, while eating his own breakfast. He loved looking into her eyes and sending her love while she looked back at him and did the same.

As they often did, he and Livvie were having oatmeal. To Livvie, oatmeal served several purposes. It was, of course, food. It was also a toy, a projectile, a floor or table covering, an art medium—among probably other, as yet, undiscovered, purposes.

"Open wide, Liv," he said. Livvie eyed the filled spoon coolly. C3's phone rang. He let it go to voice mail.

"Come on, Liv." C3 used his silly-cartoon coaxing-the-baby voice.

Livvie looked at him, then at the spoon, then again at him. She smiled faintly but didn't open her mouth.

"Watch the airplane," C3 said, making growling noises he hoped sounded airplane-like. He lowered the spoon to the tabletop. "The airplane's taking off!" The spoon gained speed and was soon airborne. "And it's in the air! It's flying! It's flying! It's …" The spoon headed for Livvie's mouth.

"It's zooming in for a landing!"

Livvie laughed and opened her mouth. She loved this game.

Once she'd eaten, C3 listened to the phone message while he ate his own oatmeal.

Billy wanted him to call.

After putting away the dishes and cleaning the table, he focused briefly on the clacking of keys from the bedroom, where Sarah was typing. He laid Livvie on the living room floor and returned Billy's call.

"Got a few minutes, C?" Billy said.

"I do."

"I don't know if I ever told you this, but when I was little, my baby sister was kidnapped and murdered."

"Shit. You alluded to something traumatic, but you never got into the details."

"Yeah," Billy said, his voice shaky. "Well, this thing impacted every part of my life. It tore my parents apart. I was ten at the time, and she was seven, and since then I've never, ever felt safe. I've never felt that comfort and love a kid is supposed to feel as part of a safe environment. You know what made me feel safe and comforted?"

"Being high?"

"Exactly."

"Yeah, but think it through, Billy. It worked for a while, but then it stopped working didn't it?"

"Yeah, I guess. It turned on me, yeah." He was starting to cry. "Everything turns on me!"

"Where are you, Billy?"

Billy gave him the address.

"I'm coming. I'm going to pick you up and bring you to my job at the counseling center. They have meetings here for clients a few times a day, and you'll be able to sit in on at least one of those. You'll be around people who love you. I'm coming, Billy."

An hour later they were together at a meeting, laughing with a speaker who shared an experience that was so much like Billy's that they just had to laugh.

• • •

Emily Ashford lived on the third floor of a brick apartment building a few blocks north of Sunrise Highway in the town of Florville, a twenty-minute ride north of Beach City.

She answered the door with a shy smile, her eyes narrow, her blonde hair, which fell around her shoulders, streaked with a darker shade of blonde. She wore navy slacks and a bird's-egg-blue cotton top. A black-and-white cat peeked from behind her ankles.

They sat down in an ivory-colored living room adorned with oil paintings of sailboats and fishing boats on the ocean and smaller waterways.

"Did you do these?" Missy asked.

Emily brightened. "I did!"

Dora and Missy looked around, scanning the paintings.

"They're very good," Dora commented.

"Thanks. Painting keeps me sane." The cat jumped into her lap as she spoke. "This is Spots. He's my love."

"We've been to visit your father," Missy began.

Emily's features fell as if pulled by gravity, and her face reflected a deep sadness. "My father's poor heart is broken." Her mouth twisted with grief. "And so is mine."

"But you didn't visit Julian," Dora said. "Is that correct?"

Emily nodded slowly. "I agreed, insisted really, that we remain apart since his birth—for both our sakes. Doesn't mean I didn't love him, though—or that I don't still. My father helped him build a Facebook page for himself—but it was really for me. So I could see him."

"You loved him from afar." Missy's words came out as a statement but were meant as confirmation.

Emily leaned forward. "He was my son!" Her narrow eyes widened and teared.

"I hope it's okay to ask," Dora began, "but when you gave him up— was that because you felt you had to?"

The woman sighed and sat back. "It was for so many reasons. I knew he was special and that taking care of him was going to be a life's work —and I wasn't up to it. Maverick insisted."

"That you give him up?" Missy asked.

Emily nodded. "He was adamant. He would have preferred an abortion, but I just couldn't."

"We'd hoped," Dora said, changing tacks, "to ask about your father."

"What would you like to know?"

"We understand he was angry at Mason Montgomery," Dora continued.

Emily scoffed. "Who wasn't? The man guaranteed he'd keep his facility running, then changed his mind. I mean, he gets to change his mind, I guess—but his choice impacted a lot of people in a pretty negative way." She leaned forward again. "He built and funded a magnificent place that improved the lives of so many people. And he promised to keep it going—it was going to be his legacy. And what a legacy it would have been!" She gave a rueful, sad grimace. "Of course, my father's pissed. A lot of people are."

Dora looked steadily at the blonde woman. "I'm just going to go ahead and ask. Is it possible your father tried to kill Montgomery—to shoot him, missed him, and accidentally killed Julian?"

Emily stared at Dora. "You think my father killed my son? That's crazy!"

Dora shrugged. "Had to ask. Something happened. Something crazy. And your father was angry at Montgomery, and Montgomery was right next to Julian ..."

Emily blinked. "Let me tell you about my father. Yes, he's angry. Really, really angry. But it's anger born of love, born of outrage. He took my son in when I didn't know where else to turn, and he loved that boy —that special, special boy who grew into such a fine, talented, sweet, oh-so-brave young man. And the fear, the terror, that Julian wouldn't be cared for was too much for him. My father was overwhelmed, consumed with the notion that Julian might not be safe. I don't think he wanted

Montgomery dead. I think he wanted Montgomery accountable! So, to answer your question, no, I don't think it's possible. Next question."

Missy said, "Tell us about your relationship with your ex-husband."

Emily looked back at Missy, her expression still sad, but this was a different kind of sadness. "I was in love with Maverick. Really, deeply in love. We were sort of obsessed with each other. Early on, we were a perfect couple—or so I thought." She grinned. "You couldn't keep us off each other. I adored him, and he adored me. And he seemed so understanding, so compassionate, so loving. We finished each other's sentences. He said I was his soulmate, and I believed him. I *was* his soulmate." She looked around and wrung her hands. "It's bewildering. He was this wonderful person." She paused and was still, then looked at Dora and Missy. "And then he changed."

"How did he change? Why did he change?"

Emily blinked. "I— I don't know. But it was gradual. At first, he seemed just a touch less into me. A touch less intimate and loving. And then he was cold. He would startle me with unkind comments that came out of nowhere." She sat back, and her eyes drifted to a painting of a wharf on which two people were fishing while a man with a beige hat with a brim was walking with a tackle box, rod, and reel, and a net over his shoulder. The water beyond the wharf was choppy—green and blue waves were dotted with whitecaps. Two birds fought for a bit of clam in the foreground.

Dora and Missy both watched her carefully.

"What did you do?" Dora asked.

"He scared me," Emily admitted, her eyes narrowing. "I pulled back, and that seemed to really piss him off."

"Did he ever see Julian during any of this time?" Missy asked.

Emily shook her head, and her bottom lip protruded. "Never."

"Did he want to see Julian?" Missy asked.

Emily shook her head again. "He never seemed to care very much about Julian one way or the other."

"Did you start seeing someone else?" Dora asked.

Startled, Emily looked sharply at Dora. "Why would you ask that?"

Dora shrugged. "Just trying to get a clear picture."

Missy added, "And it's important to know if anyone else is in danger."

Emily was taken aback. "You think I could be in danger?"

Dora shook her head. "We're just covering all the standard bases."

"Well, I did start seeing someone. His name's Robert. I'm still seeing him—a local lawyer. A good one, I understand."

"That wouldn't be Robert Bishop?" Dora asked. "He's a good local attorney we happen to know."

Emily's eyebrows went up. "Yes, it would be."

"Did Maverick find out about your new relationship?"

"You know, it's funny you should ask that. He did, but not because I told him. He just somehow knew. I didn't talk about it on Facebook, but we did go to a few restaurants. So maybe someone told him—a bartender? A waitress?"

Dora and Missy looked at one another. Dora asked, "What was Maverick's reaction?"

Emily sighed. "At first, cold shoulder. Then sarcasm. Then, he just shut me out."

Chapter 18

The family had finished Sunday afternoon dinner and were sitting around Charlie and Christine's table, sipping drinks and watching the surfers on the beach below.

"All I'm saying," Sarah explained, her voice low, "is that America isn't a level playing field. It's never been a level playing field. From the Pilgrims getting off the Mayflower and ripping off Native Americans to the slave owners, to—"

"Will you stop with that woke crap?" Charlie snapped, gesturing so emphatically with his glass that some of his single malt spilled. "Oh shit!" He clutched his glass with its valuable contents close to his chest. "Your argument is outdated. Nowadays, anybody can make enough money to be self-sufficient—you work hard, you're savvy, you do it right, and you can amass plenty of cash and live well—whether you're Black, Puerto Rican, Irish, Filipino, Chinese, Korean or what have you. America is still the land of opportunity. You just have to do it right."

Sarah nodded emphatically. "Well, yeah. Just about anyone can make it if they're a big enough asshole."

Charlie sat back, digesting what she said. "Well, there's some truth to that. You have to be competitive, and you have to win."

Christine, who'd been in the bathroom, stepped into the dining room and beckoned to Sarah. "Could you come here a minute?"

"Sure." Sarah stood and turned to Charlie. "Watch your granddaughter for a second, 'k?"

Charlie walked around the edge of the table and knelt next to Livvie, whose blue eyes watched him with interest. "Paw-paw's here," he said. "All is well. Yes! All is well! Paw-paw's here!"

Sarah followed Christine into the bathroom. Once inside, Christine turned to her and said, "I'm spotting—and I'm freaking out."

Sarah nodded. "Spotting means you need to call your obstetrician."

Christine gave a small nod; Sarah could see the fear in her eyes, which were now filled with tears.

"You just noticed it now?" Sarah asked.

Christine nodded. "Earlier today. I spent from then to now praying. Should I go to the hospital?"

Sarah's eyes wandered as she thought about this. "Do you think you should?"

"Maybe. To be safe."

"Okay then." She stepped into the hallway. "Charlie!" She walked to the dining room and found Charlie with Livvie in his arms, dancing in front of the window and singing "Pretty Woman" extremely off-key. "Charlie, take your wife to the hospital."

Charlie handed Livvie to Sarah. "Really? Is the baby okay?"

Sarah gave him a hard look. "Just take her."

Charlie rushed from the room and returned, one arm around Christine's shoulder, the other at her other elbow. "Easy now," he said, "take your time."

"I can fucking walk, Charles!" She shook herself free.

Charlie let go of Christine but kept his arms hovering around her, in just-in-case mode. "Are you kidding? You just said 'fucking.' This isn't good," he moaned. "Oh, this isn't good!"

As they approached the apartment door, it opened. C3 came in, took one look at Christine, and said, "Is everything okay? Is the baby—"

"Everything's fine," Charlie replied in a no-nonsense tone as he ushered Christine past his son and out the door.

C3 remained standing where he was, several feet inside the door of the apartment, looking after his father and Christine as they made their way to the elevator. He closed the door and walked to the living room, kissed his wife, took his daughter from her, and nuzzled her face with his nose. "How's my little Livvie!" He kissed her cheek and turned back to Sarah. "I heard something at my NA meeting I gotta run by you."

Sarah raised an eyebrow. "Are you sure you should?"

"No. I'll know if I tell you and you say I shouldn't have told you." He paused. "A guy at the meeting was talking about his disabled son. This guy talks about his son all the time. He really loves this kid."

"So far, you shouldn't have told me. Some guy loves his kid—"

"Would ya wait? He's been sharing for maybe six weeks now that his son—his disabled son—is in love with a woman—a disabled woman —at their facility."

They were standing next to the couch. Sarah sat down. He had her attention now.

C3 sat down next to her, Livvie still in his arms, her face pressed to his chest. "So his son's in love with this woman, and he's been sharing that it's the most wonderful thing."

Sarah moved her hand in a get-to-the-point circle. "And?"

"And the woman broke his son's heart because she loves someone else. And he shared at the meeting that he wants to kill that guy—the guy this girl prefers over his son."

No one spoke for a full minute. Sarah said, "You heard this? Just now?"

C3 shook his head emphatically. "I heard it two weeks ago and forgot about it."

Sarah rolled her eyes and sighed. "Charrrles!" she groaned.

C3 widened his eyes and held both palms out. "It was just something a guy said about his feelings. And I remembered it just now because he hasn't been at the meeting since then."

Sarah's eyes wandered away from C3, then snapped back to him. "You need to tell Dora."

• • •

Dora and Missy were on their living room floor, rubbing the bellies of their respective dogs, both of whom were on their backs, paws in the air, in their own versions of heaven.

The downstairs buzzer sounded, and the two women looked at one another.

"I'll get it," Missy said and stood to hit the intercom's talk button. His massage over, Comfort flipped to his feet and glared at Missy.

"Yes?" she said into the intercom.

"It's C3. I was hoping to talk to Dora."

Missy let go of the button and looked at Dora, her eyebrows raised.

Dora pursed her lips and nodded slowly. "Let him in."

Moments later, Dora held the door as C3 stepped inside and hugged her with both arms. He was dressed in a red tank top and beige shorts.

"Missed you," he said.

Dora gave a half smile. "What's up?" She nodded toward the couch. "Okay if Missy stays?"

"Absolutely." C3 sat down on the couch and explained to Dora and Missy what he'd heard and observed at the NA meeting.

When he was finished, he added, "I thought it made sense to tell you guys. Not sure it's a go-to-the-cops sort of thing."

As C3 was speaking, Dora folded her arms across her chest. When he was finished, she glanced at Missy. "What do you say we pay Fred Chase a visit?"

Ten minutes later, Missy was watching Dora as she drove. "You still mad at C3 and Sarah? And Charlie and Christine?"

Dora's mouth twisted, and she flushed with embarrassment. She raised an eyebrow and shrugged. "When you put it like that, I don't know." She shook her head, wanting to steer clear of the subject.

Missy waited for an answer, but moments later they parked in front of the forest green house with its lime green shutters and the subject was officially closed.

Fred Chase answered his door looking surprised but pleased. "What can I do for you?" He stepped back, allowing Dora and Missy inside. "C'mon in. Have a seat."

The two women sat on the sofa. Chase sat on an ottoman and leaned forward, elbows on his knees, his expression eager.

"We asked you something when we were last here," Dora began, "which I don't believe you answered."

"Okay."

"Were you angry—or rather how angry were you—about the attention Penny showed toward Julian Lockhart?"

Missy nodded. "We know William's feelings were hurt, and it would be understandable for you, as his father, to be angry—maybe toward Penny and maybe even toward Julian."

Chase's expression darkened and shuttered. "Someone hurts my boy, and sure, I get upset." The warmth in his eyes had vanished. "My job is to take care of William—and that includes his emotional well-being. He has a simple view of things. He feels in primary colors."

"What about you?" Dora asked.

"What about me?"

"How angry were you at Julian?" she continued.

He snorted a laugh. "Well, I didn't kill him!"

"Were you there?" Missy asked.

"What do you mean?"

"She means," Dora added, "were you at the event at which Julian Lockhart was killed?"

Chase stared at them; his lips tightened. "No, I was not."

"Really? You missed your son's performance?" Dora exclaimed.

"Right."

"Where were you?" Missy asked.

"That's none of your business. And I think we're done here."

• • •

As they got into the turbo and were buckling their seat belts, Dora's phone trilled. She looked to see who it was, then turned to Missy. "Like father, like son." She transferred the call to the car's hands-free.

"Hello, Charlie."

"You need to listen," Charlie sounded frantic. "Christine's at the hospital."

"What? Why? Is she okay? Is it the baby?"

"We don't know. We were at home, and she had some spotting, but we don't know the severity yet. She's with an ob-gyn now. Look, I'm sorry to bother you. I'm just freaking out and need to talk to someone before my head explodes. I have this pint of Jack Daniels that was stashed in my car for emergencies, and I'm in the ER, with that bottle down my pants, taking swigs when no one's looking." He made a swallowing sound. "How are you guys? It's been too long."

Missy was looking at Dora and mouthing, "Let's go."

Dora nodded and said, "We're on our way."

· · ·

They walked into the room at the hospital and found Christine sitting up in a hospital bed, wearing two gowns—one that closed in front, another that closed in back. An IV was taped to the back of her left hand. Holding her other hand and sitting on the bed on her right side was Charlie, who seemed to Dora to be admirably relaxed and more than a little buzzed.

C3 and Sarah were sitting on chairs against a wall opposite the foot of the bed; on the floor next to Sarah was a car seat in which Livvie was sitting, her eyes glued to her mother's face.

Christine's expression when she saw Dora and Missy walk through the door was one of surprise and delight. "You didn't have to come!"

"Of course we did!" Missy cried.

Dora nodded and smiled. "Yeah, we did." She covered Christine's and Charlie's clasped hands with one of hers.

Christine's expression was beatific and relieved. "And I'm so glad you're here."

"How are you?" Dora asked quietly. "How's—"

"She's fine," Charlie interrupted.

"How's that pint doing?" Dora asked, and Charlie looked away, embarrassed but still smiling, while C3 looked annoyed.

Charlie said, "I just need to pay extra attention to Christine's well-being for the foreseeable future."

Christine said to Dora, "And I have to apologize for not inviting you to Livvie's birthday. I'd intended it to be just family, and it kind of organically expanded to Vanessa because she works for Charles at the office and is looking for answers about Buster. Sarah's been helping her." She sighed. "I guess I've sort of neglected my main cadre of friends." She covered Dora's hand with hers. "I'm so sorry."

Dora's eyes teared, and she awkwardly leaned over and hugged Christine, who, when they disengaged, patted her hair. "I must look a mess! No makeup, and my hair …"

Dora smiled and Charlie laughed.

Chapter 19

"That's the problem with today's investigators," Thelma was saying from the doorway. "You're using Facebook as a source of investigatory information."

"And that's bad?" Missy raised an eyebrow as she scanned the local groups. "People narrate their lives on Facebook, so why not use the tools provided to us by one of the most-utilized private information contractors on the planet to look at the behavior of our targets? Not a thing wrong with that."

"I'll tell you what's wrong with that," Thelma remonstrated. "It's bullshit."

"Nope," Missy countered. "Thank you for that scientific analysis."

Dora grinned and called to Thelma. "I'm rubbing off on her!"

"Just what we need," Thelma grumbled.

Dora was at her computer, scanning local groups and contacts on Twitter and Instagram, while Adam was typing up notes at his desk.

"Ah, here you go," Dora said, reading. "Here's a thread—deep one too—claiming that there's someone out there targeting people with special needs because they're not good enough or able enough to be part of 'normal' society."

Thelma blew a Bronx cheer. "Stupid bullshit, I'm telling you. Today's equivalent of a party line—a high-tech rumor mill. You can't trust that as a source."

Dora chuckled. "Party lines are high tech?"

"For their era, yup," Thelma announced.

"What reason do they give," Missy asked, "for someone wanting to go after people with special needs?"

"You know the reason," Dora answered. "The notion that they're not good enough to be part of what these people think is normal society."

Adam glanced their way. "I'd like to hear what you've got so far on the Lockhart case." He sat back, waiting and tapping his fingers.

Dora tapped several keys on her computer keyboard and scanned her screen. "We have Julian Lockhart, a talented young man with special needs, performing at the Montgomery Special School. As he's belting out his song, he's shot by persons unknown through a window that leads to an obscured area outside the auditorium."

Missy continued, "Geller Investigations was hired several days later by the boy's father, Maverick Lockhart. The boy had been living with his grandfather."

Adam said, "Why not the parents?"

"His father's business interests don't allow him the time or focus to care for him," Missy answered.

"The mother?" Adam asked.

"The parents are estranged. The mother gave him up at birth," Dora answered. "She knew he would have special needs but the science couldn't say what they were, and right there that was too much for her. She didn't feel she could care for a child with special needs, yet she couldn't go through with an abortion."

"Which the father would have wanted," Missy added. Dora nodded in agreement.

"Enemies?" Adam asked.

"Well, the boy had none," Missy said.

"Not exactly true," Dora said. "A girl with special needs had a crush on Julian, while another guy, William Chase, had a crush on her."

Adam squinted. "So, Chase is a suspect?"

Dora shook her head. "If anyone, it would be Chase's father, who, interestingly, wasn't at the performance."

"And, I'm guessing, was unaccounted for," Adam finished. "What else?"

"The victim's guardian was his maternal grandfather, Jack Ashford, who's part of a group of parents and families of Montgomery attendees who are upset because the school's founder promised to keep the school open, and, the way they see it, has gone back on his word."

Adam stroked his chin. "Interesting, but what does that have to do with Julian Lockhart being shot?"

"When he was shot," Dora explained, "Mason Montgomery—"

"The founder," Missy said.

"—had ascended the stage and was about to hand Julian an award," Dora finished.

"You're saying someone might have targeted the founder and missed," Adam said.

"Right," Missy confirmed.

"And that someone might have been the boy's own grandfather, tragically killing his own grandson." Adam was nodding to himself. "Was the grandfather present at the event? Was he seen?"

Dora nodded. "He was the first person on stage. His grandson died in his arms."

"I see," Adam said. "So the grandfather or some like-minded individual hired someone to kill the founder, and that person missed and killed the kid. So they hired a crappy marksman as a hitman. Far-fetched. What else?"

"Possibly relevant are a group of NIMBY residents who don't want the school there," Dora pointed out.

"Okay," Adam said.

"A Montgomery senior admin in charge of security called in sick on the day of the murder," Dora added.

"Well," Adam said grimly, "if you were going to arrange for a murder at a school assembly, it might make sense to ensure that the head of security wouldn't be around."

"Exactly," Dora said.

Missy added, "We've also got a lot of noise on social media and in the press about people with special needs being unwelcome."

"In Beach City, you mean?" Adam asked.

"Well," Missy said, "in general."

"As in someone, singular or plural, is pushing the notion that disabled people might be the targets of violence," he said.

"Perhaps," Dora ventured.

Adam was looking at Dora, his expression showing he was intrigued. "What does Maverick Lockhart do for a living?"

Dora thought for a moment. "Business interests of some sort—investments, I'd assumed. Why?"

"Let's say his business is somehow shady, or some of his connections are. Great way to get to a shady guy—through his kid."

"I guess because he came to us," Missy ventured, "we assumed he'd be in the clear."

Adam shook his head. "More assumptions. And he may be in the clear, yet still be a target."

"We'll look into his work," Dora promised. "And his contacts."

Adam looked at Missy, then Dora. "My two cents, ladies—this was an intentional, targeted attack. Hard to believe a professional would miss the founder and kill this kid. Equally hard to believe anyone's targeting kids with special needs per se."

• • •

Sarah arrived home and found C3 on the living room floor next to Livvie, who was in her car seat. His face was close to hers, and he was saying, "I love you, little girl," over and over and touching her nose on the word *you.*

"Hey," Sarah said.

"Hey," he said back. "How's my girl?"

She smiled faintly, took a deep breath, and bubbled her lips on the out-breath. "The truth is, I'm overwhelmed between this little girl and my job and being your wife." She sat down next to him on the floor.

C3 took her hand, brought it to his lips, and kissed it. "You're doing great."

"No," she said, "I'm not. I feel really guilty."

"What for?"

"For …" She looked into her lap, then back at C3. "For maybe regretting having a child."

He didn't move. Just looked into her eyes. "Really?"

She looked up at the ceiling to her left and then her right. "I mean some of this is that *The Chronicle*'s been in a financial tailspin, and—"

"Isn't LaChance helping with that?"

"He was. He is. Oh shit, I forgot. He texted me that he's on his way over here!"

"When?"

"Any minute. But look. It's okay. I'm fine. Never mind. It's all good." She stood up and straightened her papers. She'd just started for the bedroom to retrieve her computer when C3 stopped her.

"Sar—"

She turned.

"Do you really regret having Livvie?"

She pressed her lips together. "I'm just overwhelmed. It's just a lot."

"What can I do?"

The downstairs buzzer sounded. "You're fine. Let me get my computer. That's LaChance." She buzzed him in.

C3 called after her. "I'm putting Livvie to bed! Try to keep your voices down." He carried his daughter in her car seat to the bedroom.

The apartment bell rang. "Be right there!" Sarah called, then she answered the door, computer in hand. LaChance was standing in the hallway in a blue sports jacket, dress shirt, and slacks, along with two other well-groomed men.

"I brought my street crew along," LaChance said.

"Okay," Sarah said cautiously. "Come in, but please speak softly. C3's just put the baby to sleep."

"How's my man doing?"

She turned as she led the way to the dining room and offered a smile. "Pretty well, actually. Make yourselves at home," she said, and everyone did.

"This is Big Ru and his brother, Little Ru Paulson," LaChance said.

Sarah smiled at the two newcomers. Big Ru had a small, tight Afro; wide-set, intelligent eyes; a broad, flat nose; and a friendly smile. His features were tightly controlled, as though the muscles of his face were clenched. Little Ru looked like Big Ru, but with bigger hair, a somewhat broader face, and a more relaxed manner—and, he was a head shorter than his brother.

"Are you guys in the news business?" Sarah asked.

The brothers looked at LaChance, who laughed. "Little Ru and his wife, Eunice, own a construction company. Big Ru is a plumber who mostly works for his brother."

"Oh." Sarah nodded. "Why do they call you Ru?"

"Our nicknames come from us being in trouble all the time," Little Ru said.

Big Ru finished his thought. "And our grandmother, Molly, was always sayin' we would rue the day we did whatever it was we were doin'."

"And did you?" Sarah asked.

"Did we what?" Big Ru asked.

"Did you rue the day you did whatever you were doing?"

The brothers looked at one another and laughed. "I don't think so," said Little Ru.

"Nah," said his brother.

"So, how are you going to help us?" Sarah asked.

"Okay," LaChance said. "My friends are here to help us increase readership. Let us do our thing, and you'll see what I'm talking about." He turned to the brothers. "I explained in the car what we're looking for —forums and threads talking about how we don't need developmentally disabled people around."

"Yep," said Big Ru. "So, let's record the meeting."

LaChance took out his phone, found the voice memo app, and started recording.

"Let's start with stories about how so many people with disabilities aren't really as disabled as they're sayin'." Big Ru said, sitting back and tapping his fingers on the table. "People with handicapped parking hangers who don't really need them, who take parking from other people."

"From the rest of us," Little Ru added.

"That's good!" LaChance looked impressed.

Sarah disagreed. "That's crazy."

"There's truth in that," Big Ru told her.

"Well, I suppose—"

Little Ru had another idea. "I think we need some stories complaining specifically about some of the disabled people at the Montgomery School."

"Like what?" LaChance asked.

"Maybe something about tax breaks, or some way they're not paying their fair share, or maybe that people with disabilities are at a starting point that's further along than everyone else."

Big Ru pointed a finger. "Unfair compensation!"

LaChance was nodding. "Interesting."

"We were talking about something else before," said Little Ru. "Along a different line. Didn't we want to have a crowd of people complaining 'bout how the shooter missed Mason Montgomery? Like he was the target and too bad they missed, and something has to be done about this guy. He committed to helping people, and he pulled his money out—he flip-flopped. He said he put it in his will, right? And he didn't. I think we need three or four letters about that."

LaChance turned to Sarah. "See how a handful of letters to the editor and some targeted social media posts can attract readers?"

Sarah was shaking her head. "I don't agree with any of this!"

LaChance waved a chiding finger. "That's the beauty of it. Of course, you don't agree. So what do you do? You write an editorial, which you then post to social media that says you don't agree. You get your point of view out there. That stirs more people up—more letters! We're providing you with a vehicle that will do that. More controversy, more readers, more advertising, and you've made your point. Voilà!"

Chapter 20

"I just finished the searches on Lockhart's name," Missy said, looking up from her computer screen at Dora, who'd been sifting through increasingly disturbing social media posts.

"And?"

"His name is associated with a half dozen assaults, quite a bit of loan sharking, and possible racketeering."

"Well, well, well. Chalk one up for Adam."

"It's interesting," Missy noted. "He seems to suddenly show up as an owner or part owner of properties—most of them small and commercial."

"What about taxes?" Dora asked. "Does he pay them?"

Missy smiled and shook her head. "Nope. At least not until he gets caught. He was found guilty of federal tax evasion two years ago and has since then made restitution, including penalties." She read silently from her screen for a moment. "Then I ran into a bit of a wall. He has an association with a dentist—one of these sudden ownerships of a piece of commercial real estate where this dentist has an office. The dentist, name of Natelson, attempted and failed to secure financing for dental equipment. Now he suddenly has the equipment, and guess who now owns a piece of his building."

"Where's the wall?" Dora asked.

"I'd like to talk to the guy, but he won't take my call."

Dora nodded slowly. "What're his hours? Is he in now?"

Missy pulled up the dentist's website. "He does seem to be, according to his listed hours."

Fifteen minutes later, Dora and Missy had parked in front of the dental practice of Douglas Natelson and made their way into the waiting room.

"We're here to see Dr. Natelson," Dora announced to the receptionist.

"Just sign the list," said the receptionist, pointing with a pen.

"No need. We just need a minute of his time."

"Well," the receptionist stammered. "If you don't have an appointment …"

Dora folded her arms and looked around the waiting room. Besides herself and Missy, there was a middle-aged Asian man in a blue T-shirt and jeans shorts, a woman with a boy of about ten, and a dark-skinned man in his twenties with jet-black hair.

"We'll just be a minute."

"I'm sorry," the receptionist said. "You'll have to make an appointment."

"We're investigating the murder of Julian Lockhart. Maybe you heard about it?"

The receptionist looked back at Dora, her expression blank.

"The murdered boy's father does business with your boss," Dora continued. "We think the father might have helped Dr. Natelson secure the money for some of his equipment. But something about that," Dora said with a wince, "doesn't seem quite kosher."

The woman with the ten-year-old was listening and beginning to look concerned. She leaned toward Dora. "Why don't you take our spot? We were next, but we can come back another time."

"Why, thank you," Dora said, gratefully. "But we'd rather not take a patient's spot. I'm sure Dr. Natelson will find a minute for us."

The dentist had stepped into the receptionist's area and was looking at a list of patients and glancing at Dora. The receptionist whispered something to him. He pressed his lips together and nodded to Dora and Missy.

"Why don't you come on back." He looked at his remaining patients. "We'll just be a minute."

Dora and Missy stepped into one of the examination rooms. Dora looked around at the equipment. "Very nice, Dr. Natelson. We won't keep you. We're investigating the murder of Maverick Lockhart's son, Julian."

"Who?" The dentist looked baffled.

"The man who helped finance your dental equipment. We were wondering what you could tell us about him."

"Oh." The dentist's expression changed to one of resignation. "There's not much I can tell you, really. Maverick Lockhart's a lifesaver. I needed some help, and I got word through some friends that he was the man to see. He helps small businesses."

"And then he owns them," said Missy.

Natelson shrugged. "He does require collateral. But that's just good business." He looked at Dora. "He's been a big help. I needed help, and he helped me."

"At what rate of repayment?" Dora asked.

Natelson said, "I think we're done here. I have no complaints about the man. I needed help, and he helped me out. He's a benefactor. Maybe even an angel."

· · ·

Ganderson was sitting at his desk, eating potato chips out of a bag. Mallard was facing him at his own desk, frowning at his computer. "I think Sarah Turner over at *The Chronicle* is losing her mind."

"What do you mean?" Ganderson said as he munched on chips.

"What?"

"I asked what you meant."

"Put the chips down for a minute. Between your chewing and the crunching of that bag, I can't hear myself think, much less whatever you have to say."

"Okay." Ganderson put the bag of chips down on his desk, reached for it, took a few more chips, then flicked it away with a finger so that it was beyond his reach.

"Sarah Turner is printing letter after letter from nutjobs who don't like people with disabilities."

"What are they saying?"

"That they have unfair advantages, that some don't really have special needs, that they're gaming the system."

"Some of that's probably true." Ganderson was eyeing the chips bag. "There's no accounting for the idiots out there."

"How 'bout you throw those chips over here."

Ganderson reached for the bag, took a fistful of chips, and tossed the bag across the length of both desks. Mallard reached into the bag, came up with crumbs, and held the bag up to his eye. "You finished them, you slob."

Ganderson shrugged. "Log yourself onto Facebook. I want you to see something—I tagged you."

"With the Mrs. Lewis account?"

The two detectives used several fake accounts to peruse social media. Mrs. Amanda Lewis, a fictitious thirtysomething mother of three, was one of these.

"Okay. Hang on." Mallard logged on and scrolled down. "Oh, look at that. You're talking about the Ashford thing?"

"Yup. Grandpa Ashford's pretty vocal in that group."

"'Who's Going To Care After We're Gone?'" Mallard read. "Yeah. I get it. Only now, Grandpa doesn't have to care because the kid is gone."

"True," Ganderson said. "You know, I've been thinking about Ashford. He was right there, outside in his yard, with this sniper rifle— shooting targets, and doing so illegally."

"Yeah?"

"Hard for me to believe he's involved in this thing, even though he's been so vocal about despising Montgomery. I mean, that's the thing. He's so out in the open about everything—despising Montgomery, shooting this sniper rifle … Who would be so public about somewhat damning shit?"

Mallard shrugged. "An innocent man."

Ganderson nodded. "That's what I'm thinking."

"Or he's nuts. Or maybe," Mallard ventured, "that's what he wants us to think." Then he laughed. "Listen to this—from the mother of a kid at Montgomery. 'What really pisses me off are these woke people who tell me not to have guns around. I have a son who is disabled. I'm a single mother. Damn right I want to have guns around. Got an AR-15 right here on the wall, and a Glock in my pocketbook. If you don't like it—F-U.'"

He grinned at Ganderson, who said, "What d'you say we go over to see Lonny Dubon and ask him about that rifle Bannion was holding on to for him at the range?"

Ganderson stood up, took his brown suit jacket from the back of his chair, and slipped into it.

Once parked at Richard "Lonny" Dubon's place, Mallard led the way to the front door and found it several inches ajar. He glanced back at Ganderson, who nodded, then drew his Glock and held it in the ready position. Mallard did the same and knocked on the doorframe. "Mr. Dubon?" he called.

There was no response.

"Richard Dubon?" Ganderson called, louder.

No response.

Mallard cautiously led the way into the two-story home.

They found Richard "Lonny" Dubon several feet inside the home's foyer, lying on his side. His arms and legs were bent at impossible angles, and he had a hole about three-quarters of an inch in diameter in the center of his forehead.

• • •

Virginia Rabelson was exhausted. She'd been having trouble sleeping since the shooting at Montgomery and was finding getting out of bed to be a chore. Doing her shopping, buying gas for the car, and taking care of bills had become overwhelming burdens. She wondered if she might be depressed. She was looking forward to climbing into bed, fully dressed. She'd been too burned out recently to change into pajamas at night; she managed only to change her underpants and sometimes her bra, and as often as not, threw a sweater on over the same blouse she'd had on the day before. Now and then she took off the blouse and left the bra and sweater on. She rarely bothered to change her pants at all.

She was far too tired to pay attention to the cars behind her, and never noticed the black Chevy Blazer that had been two or three cars behind her all the way home. The Blazer parked several houses from hers. Its driver's-side door opened slowly and quietly as Virginia trudged up her walk to her door. Moments later, as she opened the door and stepped inside her house, she was grabbed from behind and forced forward, with both arms pinned behind her back.

Her assailant hadn't uttered a sound.

"What do you want?" Virginia cried. "Do you want money? I have $600 in my freezer—in the back, under some chicken thighs. Take it. Take it!"

Her assailant didn't respond. She was forced to the floor, with her right arm between her assailant's legs and her left pinned behind her by her own weight and the ground. Her right arm was yanked violently back and torn from its socket.

Virginia screamed, but her scream was cut off as a cloth was shoved into her mouth and down into her throat so that she gagged. Her assailant then focused on her left arm—forcing it, too, backward until it was yanked from its socket, then broken. Virginia was screaming into the cloth, but the sound came out as a muffled moan.

The attacker's hands slid down Virginia's left leg and grasped her left foot, while her torso remained in the grasp of her attacker's legs. Her foot was twisted and broken at the ankle.

Virginia passed out. Several minutes later, her attacker slapped her face until she woke up. With both her arms dislocated and her arms and ankles broken, she was in so much shock that the pain was far less than it would have been in a day or so. But she was spared that pain by her attacker, who flipped her onto her back so that she found herself looking into the cruel, gaunt face of a woman—her hair pulled back, her eyes looking at her without emotion from deep in a bony skull. The woman smiled, then grasped Virginia's head between ropey forearms and twisted, snapping her neck.

But Diana Moran wasn't finished. She stood over her victim, looking over her handiwork. Satisfied, she withdrew a small pink handgun, a Springfield XD-S, from a cross-draw holster, which had been hidden on her belt behind her long, loose-fitting blue split-neck summer top. She moved Virginia's head with her gloved hands, centering it just so within a perfectly arranged tableau, getting the composition was exactly right. Then she shot her in the center of her forehead.

• • •

Sarah and C3 were sitting on the floor of their apartment with Livvie in C3's lap. Several feet away, Vanessa sat next to Kelvin with Buster in her lap. Drew was doing his best to read the book *Goodnight Moon,* which had been read to him so many times that he knew much of it by heart.

Vanessa was explaining what had occurred at the appointment she and Buster had just returned from. Kelvin had gone along to provide moral support. Drew had stayed with Sarah, C3, and Livvie.

"She gave us a sheet with a lot of information, and you're welcome to read it, but I'd just as soon not have to look at it right now. It's depressing." No one said anything, so Vanessa continued. "Eventually, they're going to want to have a team evaluate Buster."

"That's right," Kelvin said. "A speech pathologist, an occupational therapist, a psychologist …"

Sarah looked surprised. "A psychologist?" She looked at Kelvin, who shrugged.

"They want to cover as many bases as possible," he explained.

"And get this," Vanessa said, her forehead creasing. "The fact that he's now been diagnosed as being on the spectrum doesn't guarantee he'll get services."

Sarah sat back. "How can that be?"

"No idea," Vanessa answered, looking dejected. "Wait." She had a black pocketbook on a strap over her shoulder. She opened it and took out a printed sheet of paper from which she read. "Buster will still need to be 'evaluated by the school system to show that he meets eligibility requirements to receive services.'"

"Let me see that." Sarah took the paper from Vanessa and read it, frowning. She flipped the paper over. "Did you read this side—the list of symptoms with check marks for those that apply to Buster?"

Vanessa nodded sadly. "Looks to be correct."

Sarah read aloud. "'Does not respond to their name by twelve months. Does not point to objects to show interest by fourteen months.

Avoids eye contact and wants to be alone. Has delayed speech and language skills. Gets upset by minor changes in environment.' Then there are things listed that don't apply to Buster."

As Sarah read, Vanessa waved the list away, and her eyes filled with tears. Her cheeks clenched, and she began to cry, hugging Buster to her.

Chapter 21

Ganderson blew out a breath, puffing his cheeks, then ran a hand back over his hair and fumbled in his pocket for a tissue with which to wipe the hair product from his palm. "How 'bout we both take a week in Tahiti?"

"Right," Mallard said. "Er, ah— Why don't you ask Stalwell for the time? Tell me how it goes, okay?" He watched the exhaustion play out in his partner's expressions and body language. The day had been crazy and trying—a relentless, one-after-the-other march of stressful, unnecessary criminality.

Mallard didn't need a vacation. He needed a drink. He needed a half dozen drinks. He looked again at Ganderson, wondering if he would agree to a few quick ones at one of the local gin joints—Rudy's maybe.

The day had begun and ended with similar-sounding wackos waving weapons in the general vicinity of the Montgomery Special School, spurred on perhaps—with certainty in one case—by recent letters in *The Chronicle* or posts on social media: a forty-year-old with a Glock and a grudge who watched far too much of certain news channels and paid far too much attention to certain social media outlets; and just now, a kid with a rifle who—luckily—had posted his armed status and location on social media.

Good job turning yourself in, kid. The kid had also re-shared a news article about Julian Lockhart's murder. *Was that what Lockhart had been —some nutjob driven wild by news or social media?*

Far more stressful were these murders—two of them—and the more he and Paul researched, the more connections between them seemed to spring up and lead to additional, even more troubling, information.

First was Virginia Rabelson, who'd been physically torn apart by at least one, perhaps several trained assassins. Her limbs and neck had been broken, and she'd been shot in the forehead at close range by a 9 mm handgun. Then, Richard "Lonny" Dubon, who'd been killed in a similar manner. These facts had been gathered during the first half of what had been a very long day.

The second half had been even more exhausting. For nearly five hours, they'd navigated databases, police files, news reports, court records, photos, their own notes, and whatever scraps of information they could coax from their colleagues, looking for connections between the cases.

What had emerged was a still blurry picture of relationships.

Virginia Rabelson had worked in accounting at the Montgomery School.

She was also employed as a private contractor by several establishments that had benefited from off-the-record "loans" from Maverick Lockhart—the same Maverick Lockhart whose son, Julian, had been murdered at the Montgomery School mid-song just several weeks earlier. Richard "Lonny" Dubon was a low-life thief and street thug who'd been in and out of trouble with the law for decades. He'd been incarcerated for a handful of misdemeanors and two class C felonies—both assaults.

Was there some direct connection between the two murders? Perhaps, but not as yet borne out by facts.

Research demonstrated Dubon's association with a half dozen other known criminals, none of whom could be connected to Rabelson.

Mallard scanned his meta notes—notes he'd taken summarizing more specific, in-depth notes from multiple sources. He said, "So, we've got Dubon running up a drug tab, then working off his debt and making some kind of living as a low-level muscle-for-hire."

Ganderson ran his palm over his face, then looked at his hand, realizing that he'd again run it through his product-laden hair. "Yee-ahhh. That's about right."

"And who would you say he worked *for*?"

"He's part of a network," Ganderson replied. "Bunch of knuckleheads who hang out in the back of Mae's Diner late mornings—except when they're alone, when they sit at her counter. Haven't talked to Pearlie Mae yet for details, or Winnie Chambers, for that matter."

Winnie was Pearlie Mae's partner and wife; they shared ownership of the diner. "They hang out at any number of bars later in the day. My guess is, when anyone in that group knows someone who needs an enforcer, they come to Lonny Dubon, who was probably available for certain types of jobs."

Mallard looked at Ganderson but said nothing.

Ganderson waited and eventually said, "So, Mona Lisa, what d'ya think?"

Mallard nodded, chewing the inside of his right cheek. "Okay, far as it goes."

"How far *should* it go?"

"Maverick Lockhart."

"You have a sentence to go with the name?"

"That's who Lonny Dubon worked for—Maverick Lockhart."

Ganderson said nothing. He lifted his arm and was about to run his hand back through his hair again, but at the last moment he recalled the hair product and refrained. "So, who killed Dubon, Sherlock? Was it Maverick Lockhart—his employer?"

Mallard switched cheeks. "Well, not personally." His phone buzzed. He picked up.

"Yeah, Cathy?"

Ganderson's eyebrow went up.

"Where? Is he in the hospital? Shit. We'll be right over." He hung up, then stood, took his jacket from the back of his chair, and put it on. "Someone broke into Mason Montgomery's apartment and attacked him with a hammer."

• • •

Mallard and Ganderson walked into the offices of ML Industries, which was in an office building just off an exit of the Northern State Parkway. They hadn't called ahead, because they didn't want Lockhart to be conveniently out of the office when they arrived.

A young blonde woman in a black-and-white checkered business suit sat behind a desk in the reception area. Ganderson approached her, shield out.

"We need to see your boss."

The woman didn't look surprised. She held up a finger, stepped from behind her desk, and disappeared down a hallway. Moments later, she returned and stood to one side of the hallway's entrance.

"First door on your left."

Ganderson headed for the hallway.

"Thank you, young lady," Mallard said, with a two-finger salute.

Lockhart's office door was open; as the detectives entered, he rose from behind his desk and motioned to four chairs opposite him.

"Tracy explained that you're police officers. I like to know who I'm talking to. Do you have cards?"

The detectives proffered cards, then sat down. Lockhart looked at the cards, sat, and looked at the detectives, shaking his head. "What would two Beach City detectives want with me? I have nothing to do with Beach City."

"First of all," Mallard corrected, "you have interests in six businesses there that we know of."

Lockhart didn't disagree.

"And," Ganderson added, "until recently, a more personal connection."

"What's that supposed to mean?"

"Your son went to a treatment facility there."

Lockhart stared at Ganderson, who stared right back, widening his eyes.

Lockhart suddenly smiled. "You solved his murder? Thank God!"

"That's not why we're here," Mallard said.

"It's been several weeks. What gives?"

Ganderson said, "We're wondering what's happening to people who work for you. Two were just violently murdered. You sure you feel safe?"

Lockhart's eyebrows rose. "Did you come here to mock me?"

"You mock the law," Ganderson countered.

"I'm an honest businessman with diversified interests."

"Really?" Mallard mused. "Er, ah— What might those be?"

Lockhart shrugged. "As you just alluded to, I have interests in local businesses—small businesses—here on Long Island. I like to see our local commerce do well. It's good for our communities, our families ..."

"Fuck's sake," Mallard said, rolling his eyes.

"Running for office?" Ganderson asked.

"Wouldn't dream of it. But to answer your question, I have diverse local interests, and I also have interests overseas. The interests here are in small businesses; the interests overseas are different."

Ganderson blew out a breath. "C'mon. Among your interests here is drug distribution, and among your interests overseas is drug acquisition."

Lockhart drew his head back, a pained expression on his face. "Slander! I'm hurt that you would say such a thing! I demand to see any evidence of any of that!"

Ganderson grinned. "Slandering you's like putting lipstick on a pig."

Lockhart's expression hardened into an angry sneer. "You got some-thing to talk about? Get to it, or be on your way. I'm busy."

"We're getting to it," Ganderson said.

Mallard asked, "How is it that two people who work for you were just killed—both violently murdered—in nearly the same way?"

Lockhart looked surprised, a "who-me?" expression on his face. "No one who works for me was murdered—not that I'm aware."

"Your money launderer and your muscle."

Lockhart nodded slowly, a serene smirk on his face. "Okaaay. If you're talking about Virginia Rabelson and Richard Dubon, Rabelson was my accountant, and a good one. That's the extent I know of the work she did for me. Lonny ran occasional errands, nothing more. If either one earned a living doing anything else—hey, free country."

Ganderson laughed. "Yeah, Lonny ran errands. And sometimes beat the hell out of the people he visited on your behalf."

Lockhart looked aghast. He put a hand to his chest. "You guys give me agita. If he were around to hear it, I'd make it clear he should never do such things. If he did any of that, which I doubt, he did it on his own. Nothing to do with me. Lonny is—was—enthusiastic." He crossed himself. "God rest his soul."

Mallard snorted a laugh.

"Right," Ganderson drawled. "Well, we thought you might find it interesting that we were able to acquire a rifle that belonged to him—a rifle we can prove was the one used to kill your son."

The detectives were satisfied to see true shock dawn on Lockhart's face.

"What?"

"C'mon," Mallard wheedled. "You already knew that, didn't you? It's why you had Lonny Dubon killed."

At that moment, something in the room changed. A tension infused the air. Both detectives felt it. A woman had slipped into the room—a bony woman with sunken eyes as flat and devoid of emotion as those of any reptile. Even Maverick flinched and looked away as she walked across the room, turned, and leaned against a wall, eyeing both detectives with a chilly smile.

• • •

Dora and Missy were sitting together behind Missy's desk, looking at the spreadsheet that was part of their notes for the Julian Lockhart murder.

Missy pointed at two names, Frederick Chase and Crayton Warbler. "I don't like that these guys weren't at the assembly where Julian was killed—neither one of them. Chase's kid was in the assembly, and he happens to have a motive. And the other guy, Warbler, is just plain weird, and the fact that the attendees at Montgomery are afraid of him is creepy."

Dora looked from the screen to Missy. "We asked Chase point blank, and he said his whereabouts were none of our business." She blinked a few times, thinking. "You'd think he'd come up with something, given he'd probably want to eliminate his name from consideration."

Missy nodded. "So what are some reasons for why he wouldn't want to do that?"

Dora looked baffled. "No idea."

"How 'bout whatever he was doing was something that was even more important to keep secret than clearing his name from our investigation," Missy proposed.

"Okay, but what might that be?"

Missy raised her eyebrows. "We asked Chase. Why don't we ask Warbler?"

Dora bit the inside of her lip, thinking. "It's possible the kids at Montgomery—"

"They're not all kids."

"Right. The people, the attendees, at Montgomery are afraid of him because his tone of voice, his facial expressions seem scary. Doesn't necessarily mean he's dangerous. He's a creepy guy."

"True. But I say we ask him why he wasn't at an assembly it was his job to help protect."

"Agreed. Go for it," Dora suggested.

Missy dialed the school's number and asked for Crayton Warbler, explaining that she was investigating the Julian Lockhart murder, but neglecting to mention she wasn't a police officer. She was relieved she wasn't asked.

Finally he picked up.

"Dean Warbler."

"Missy Winters, from Geller Investigations."

Warbler gave no indication he remembered her. "Yes?"

"I won't keep you. My partner and I were in to see you recently. We're investigating Julian Lockhart's murder."

"I remember."

"We were wondering where you were when the murder occurred."

After a short silence, Warbler said, "I took off that day. I wasn't well."

"I see. Could anyone verify your whereabouts?"

"No. I, well… Yes, I suppose, if you must. But if I tell you, I must insist that you keep this information private."

Missy looked at Dora; her eyebrows went up. "I will do that unless a court of law requires that information."

Warbler sighed. "Fair enough, I suppose. But this is extremely personal."

"Go ahead."

"I was out to breakfast at that time."

"I see. And you say that can be verified?"

"Yes, by my partner. The man I was with. He's a parent of a Montgomery student, which is one of several reasons I must request as strongly as possible that this information remain private."

"I see. Who was your partner at breakfast?"

"His name is Chase. Frederick Chase."

Chapter 22

C3's phone rang. Billy. He hadn't heard from Billy in days, and seeing his name on the phone was at once terrifying and a relief. It was a relief because Billy was alive. C3 had seen so many people overdose, so many kids pick up one last bag of dope and die. So it wasn't that, unless the call was from someone else—his mother or a cop on Billy's phone.

It was terrifying because Billy hadn't been in a good place of late. He'd been through trauma as a child—suffered the loss of his baby sister—and had never felt safe ever since.

C3 took the call.

"Oh thank God, C," Billy said.

"Great to hear from you. What's up?"

"Ugh. What's not up? I've been staying with my folks. I was living with Amanda. I told you about Amanda, didn't I?"

"I don't think so."

"She's beautiful—and a beautiful person—but she's wounded, you know? Like a little, wounded bird with a broken wing or a broken heart, and I'm just not up for fixing people. I don't have it in me."

C3 wasn't sure, but Billy sound like he was crying. "You can only fix yourself," C3 said.

"I can't even do that."

"You can, with God's help."

"Don't talk to me about God. Where is God, anyway?"

"You know where to find Him." C3 put the thumb and fingers of one hand to either side of his temples. "Look, all the shit you have going on is out of your control. So let it happen. It'll pass. You'll get through it.

You've survived everything that's ever happened to you. Everything that's ever happened *to* you has been *for* you. You've stayed clean for quite a while. Isn't that a miracle? Isn't that evidence of something greater running the show?"

"I picked up."

Fuck, C3 said to himself. Then he said to Billy, "Listen. First tell me what you picked up."

"A bag of dope."

"Did you do it yet?"

"No. I just bought it."

C3 paused. He wasn't sure he believed Billy. He prayed it was true. He loved Billy, who reminded him so much of himself—a good, sweet kid whose troubles were too much for him and who sought solutions from the wrong places. He just needed to be turned toward the right places and gently prodded along the path, and perhaps held up a little bit so he wouldn't fall.

"Where are you, Billy?"

"On Dandelion Road, around the corner from the liquor store, by that empty lot."

"Did you go into the liquor store?"

"No. I was going to, but I called you instead."

"Good. You did good, Billy. Now just stay right there. Don't move. I'm on my way, right now. Remember your sister. Keep her with you. Let her keep you from doing that bag. She wouldn't want that. Can you do that for me?"

"I'll be here. For a while anyway."

C3 hung up and made sure Livvie was okay. She was sleeping on a blanket on the floor next to Sarah, who was scrolling through who-knew-what on her computer. Probably this week's articles.

He rushed out of the apartment and downstairs to the car, then drove as fast as he dared through the night toward Dandelion Street. His phone rang. He saw it was Billy, but he would be there in a minute or two, so he let it go to voice mail.

He pulled up in front of the lot on Dandelion Street, around the corner from the liquor store, and looked around. He didn't see Billy.

He walked to the liquor store and peered in the window. A woman was behind the counter, and two customers were on the other side of the counter. But no Billy. He hurried back to his car and walked a circle around it. "Bill!" he called, and looked in every direction.

No Billy.

He walked toward the lot, and something gleamed—a reflection from the streetlight in the empty lot. He took a few steps forward and squinted, but he saw nothing discernible. Just dark shapes, bushes, trash …

"Billy?"

Nothing. He stepped over the chain that hung over the curb cut and walked toward where he'd seen the light.

Billy was lying on his side.

C3 bent over him and pressed a finger to the side of his neck.

Then he dialed 911.

After ending the call, he remembered the voice mail from Billy and played it. "Hey, C. I'm really sorry. I— I don't want to be here. I— I don't like it here." He was crying. "I wanna see my sister! I'm gonna go now."

The recording ended.

C3 sat down on the curb and waited for the EMTs, his head hanging between his knees.

• • •

Dora twirled the spaghetti around her fork. "This is incredible, Miss. Very unique sauce." She took several swallows from her bottle of Bell's Two Hearted Ale, her new favorite. She enjoyed trying different brands of beer and noting the subtle differences.

Missy laughed, delighted. "I'm so glad. I use a combination of spices that reflect my different heritages."

"And those are?"

Missy's eyes looked upward as she thought. "The Polynesian islands, which are south of Hawaii, and Kunming, which is in southern China and is known as the city of eternal spring."

"Well, it's terrific."

Missy beamed. "Thank you!" She pointed, laughing. "Look at the dogs."

The dogs were sitting primly and politely, side by side, staring up at Missy, who'd brought the food to the table from the kitchen and dished it out from the serving plate.

Dora nodded in agreement. "Aw. They have such hope."

"Hope?" Missy mused. "They're radiating guilt."

Dora's phone trilled. She looked at it but didn't recognize the number. She took the call. "This is Dora."

"Hi, Dora, this is Emily Ashford. I need to meet with you."

"Why don't you start by telling me—"

"I can't. I don't trust the phone."

"Well, I'm—"

"I don't trust anything but meeting with you, and I'm not safe at home."

Dora paused. "We're having dinner now. What does tomorrow look like?"

"No, no, no. Didn't you hear me? It's an emergency! I'm not safe. Meet me as soon as you can get here. I'll be in a little green Chevy by the taxi stand in the lot at the Florville train station. Soon as you can!"

Dora's eyes flicked to Missy, who gave a little nod. "On my way."

• • •

It had been raining hard since early afternoon, and by the time Dora was driving north, the sewers were backed up and the streets were flowing with garbage blown from the tops of trash cans before the morning's garbage pickup. Dora shook her head at the garbage. Before becoming an investigator, she'd been a garbage collector and had taken pride in her work. She'd regularly bent to pick up stray trash as she made the rounds on the truck with Mo, her former partner.

As she drove, the rain abated, and by the time she arrived at the Florville train station, it had stopped entirely. The town was on one of the main Long Island east-west thoroughfares and was well-known for its variety of quality restaurants, so Dora wasn't surprised by the crowded streets and paucity of parking spaces. The spot she found was several blocks from the train station, so she enjoyed the walk and the contrast between a brightly colored sunset and the slowly retreating storm clouds.

When she knocked on the window of the little green Chevy, the blonde head inside jerked, startled. Emily unlocked the door, allowing Dora to slide into the passenger seat, whereupon she locked the doors again.

"Oh, thank God you came. I'm just freaking out!"

"Calm down. Tell me what happened." Dora did her best to exude serenity.

"I know who killed Julian."

"Okay. Who?"

"Maverick—his father."

"His father? Why would you say that?"

"Because he's a sociopath. He's been calling me nonstop for two days. He's been threatening me, and I'm pretty sure he's stalking me!"

"Why?"

"I told you. He's crazy!"

"Slow down. And back up. Tell me what happened."

Emily swallowed several times. She looked a mess. Her hair was mussed and frazzled. She was sweating and shaking. Dora was concerned for her health.

"Okay." Emily patted the air. "Okay. He used to say bad things to me —about me. Then he would deny saying them."

"Well, that sucks, but it's probably pretty common."

"I never said he was unique. Anyway, he did things, then denied doing them, and went around telling people we knew that I was crazy because I claimed he was doing things."

Dora nodded. "Gaslighting," she murmured.

"What?"

"It's called gaslighting."

"Yeah, well. I would explain that he was hurting me, and he would say these twisted things in response—things he thought were positive, like 'I'm sorry you think I hurt you.' Is that twisted, or what?"

"It's messed up, yeah, but why do you think he killed Julian?"

"He knows you're investigating."

That's right, Dora thought. *Because he's our client.* She waited.

Emily was calmer now, collecting her thoughts. "To understand why he killed Julian, you need to understand Maverick. He was obsessed with me, but he was also obsessed with himself. The only time he was happy was when he was telling me how great he was and I listened. He needs an audience. That man thinks he's the center of the universe, and he felt appreciated only when I showed appreciation. He was the sun, and I was his adoring planet that reflected his sunlight. He had to have me to shine love at him, and if he couldn't have me, no one could."

"Well, okay, but I still don't see—"

"But when I broke away, he changed. He wanted me back, and yet, at the same time, he hated me. He turned as vicious as vicious can be. He told me many times—in many phone calls—that he was going to kill me. He wanted a reaction." She shrugged. "But I didn't react, and that drove him crazy!"

Dora held up a finger. "So, let me get this straight. You think he killed Julian to get at you?"

She laughed bitterly. "I don't *think* that, I *know* that. See, I regret letting go of Julian. It was the biggest mistake of my life, and it was Maverick who convinced me to do it. He said I wouldn't be able to care for Julian. He didn't want Julian in his life, and he needed me to fawn all over him. He saw Julian as broken, inferior. He had no empathy for him—none whatever. Zero. And yet I adored Julian." Her eyes teared. "Julian was a piece of my heart, and it drove Maverick insane." She pressed her lips together and shook her head sadly. "I agreed to stay away from Julian, but I followed him on Facebook. Oh, I loved him so much. He was such a gentle, sweet soul. He was so … My son."

Dora narrowed her eyes and shook her head. "I'm still not quite getting why you're so sure he murdered Julian."

"Because he vowed, he swore, to get me—to do whatever he had to do to hurt me, to make sure I never have any happiness. To take away anything I love. That's the key. *That's* what he swore. I had a boyfriend —Jalen. We had a nice little relationship, you know? And Maverick scared him away. Jalen was a pretty tough guy in his own way. An ex-cop from Beach City."

"Would that be Jalen Scofield?"

"Yes!"

"I've met him. He was one of my instructors two years ago, during my brief tenure with the BCPD. Good guy."

"Yeah, well, Maverick went after him, threatened him. And when Jalen wouldn't listen, he sent someone who made sure he would. Some exotic killer."

Dora didn't know what to say. She did remember Officer Scofield having a bizarre accident. Now, here was Emily, doing a rather effective job of accusing Dora's client of murder.

Emily leaned toward her. "He did it. I promise you."

"Why not go to the police?"

"Because they'll never catch him. He's too smart. And because he'll find out and kill me."

"The police can't catch him—and you think I can?"

Emily held Dora's gaze. "I think he'll at least pay attention to you. He'll give you a few minutes of his time." She gave a hint of a smile. "I've heard about you."

"Yeah? What've you heard?"

"You get things done."

Dora took a deep breath. "So, what do you want me to do?"

Emily looked at her, hope in her eyes. "I want you to do your job. You're an investigator. Solve my son's murder."

• • •

A second front of clouds had rolled in, and the rain began again, so Dora stayed beneath the train tracks as she walked east toward her car. The tracks were held up by stippled gray iron pillars. As she passed one, a thin figure stepped from behind it.

"Dora Ellison?"

"Yes?"

The woman was an emaciated figure, skeletal and bony, with eyes that burned from within deep sockets.

"You need to back off the Julian Lockhart case," she said.

Now the woman had Dora's attention.

"Why?"

The woman smiled through missing teeth and, quick as lightning, grabbed one of Dora's arms, pulled Dora to her, and elbowed her in the mouth. Dora tasted the blood and spit out one of her incisors.

Who is this woman? she wondered.

Dora settled into battle mode, advancing slowly on the woman, her weight on her rear leg. Dora kicked the woman's front leg, unsettling her, then quickly kicked high, but the woman grabbed hold of her foot and shot for her plant leg, taking her down. Dora fell back into guard, and the women seemed to have an intuitive, organic understanding of the position. She began raining elbows and ground-and-pound strikes down on Dora's face.

Dora had to get out of this position. She managed to scramble to her feet and into a boxing stance, protecting her face and ribs while defending against the woman's takedowns. The woman evaded her strikes and counterstruck with such precision and force that Dora was in the odd position of having to admire her while desperately trying to survive. The woman was a jiujitsu machine, and a precise, devastating striker. Dora intuitively knew she was at a disadvantage in both circumstances— which had never happened before.

Dora jabbed and threw a right cross, followed by a double hook. She was pleased when the first of the hooks landed flush on the woman's right eye, which she knew would close.

Unfortunately, the woman somehow grabbed Dora's left hand and twisted it behind Dora's back—exquisitely painfully. The woman's strength was inhuman.

Who is she? Where did she come from? Dora wondered. She sank to her knees while spinning to her left to reverse the hold. The woman disappeared from her field of view for a second while Dora spun. She felt the hold release, then leaped to her feet.

"See you later, cookie," the woman said, then she was gone.

Dora looked around, walking in a circle while rubbing her left arm, which, she knew, was sprained, if not broken. She was bruised and battered and wanted to go home.

• • •

Once in her car, Dora set her phone up in a holder that fit into an air-conditioning vent, then drove with one hand while clutching her other arm to her side. The arm hurt, her mouth hurt, and her ribs hurt. But more than anything, her pride hurt.

She used the turbo's voice recognition ability to call Emily and make sure she was okay, which she was. She then made an excuse and got off the phone. She didn't want Emily to pick up on what had happened.

When she got home, Missy had just returned from the library and was sitting on the floor with both dogs. She took one look at Dora and flew to her side. "Were you in an accident?"

Dora shook her head.

"A fight?"

Dora nodded.

"With whom?"

Dora didn't answer but allowed Missy to lead her to the bathroom, where she started a bath and examined Dora's wounds under the light.

"You lost a tooth, which took a gouge out of the inside of your cheek. And you're going to have a hell of a shiner. Can you move your arms, legs, fingers?"

Dora did as she was asked.

"Doesn't seem as though anything's broken, though the way you're holding your arm, you might have a bone bruise or even a fracture. Possibly a broken rib. It's a good sign you can move though."

"Wonderful," Dora said.

Missy touched Dora's chin. "Hey, look at me."

Dora did.

"I'm glad you're here. I'm glad you're okay enough to be sitting here, letting me kiss you." She kissed Dora lightly on the mouth.

Dora's face contorted—her lower lip trembled and pouted outward, her nostrils flared, and she began to cry.

"Shhh." Missy carefully put an arm around Dora and hugged her for a long moment.

"I let people down," Dora said sadly.

"What? Why? No, I don't want to hear your twisted self-pity logic. You let no one down! You're working a case, and you were assaulted. What? So you're going to quit?"

Freedom was in the bathroom doorway, whining. Comfort stood between the larger dog's front paws, looking ready for battle. Dora had to laugh.

"You're now my patient, so you have to listen to me," Missy said, shaking a stern finger. "I'm going to make you some soup while you have a nice bath, then you can put on your robe." She poured much of a box of Epsom salts into the bath. "But while you have your bath, I have a meditation for you to listen to about healing physical pain."

"Yes, ma'am," Dora said, smiling through her tears.

A few minutes later, Dora was neck deep in their jacuzzi tub, the jets on low, while a meditation first relaxed her body from head to toe, then helped her visualize her pain with finite boundaries. The meditation had her give her pain a shape and a color—violet. Meanwhile, she breathed blue light up and down her spine, then breathed peace in and breathed the pain out. The meditation had her encase her pain within several geometric shapes. She did this with both her physical pain and her psychic, emotional pain.

By the end of the meditation, she was more herself, her pain was manageable, and she was ready to consider the events of the day, their bearing on the case, and next steps.

Missy's chicken noodle soup was delicious.

Dora looked at her with a curious half-smile. "So, if we got married, would that make you Jewish?"

"Excuse me, did you say married?"

Dora nodded. "You take such good care of me. I was just wondering—probably because you make such terrific homemade chicken soup —whether you'd be Jewish."

"Is that what you'd want?"

Dora's eyes twinkled. "Maybe." She turned serious. "Did you believe Emily's story about Maverick?"

"You mean that he killed his own son?" Missy thought for a moment, then slowly shook her head. "It's a little far-fetched."

Dora nodded. "And why didn't she tell us all this before?"

"She's probably trying to manipulate us into putting pressure on Maverick."

"Well, but he's our client. We work for him."

Missy nodded. "I'm aware, but she doesn't know that, and I'm glad you didn't say so."

Chapter 23

"The facility is okay with all of us joining you?" Vanessa asked. She held each of her boys by the hand as they walked down the steps into the lobby of the assisted living facility, trailed by Sarah, who was carrying Livvie's car seat with Livvie looking up at all of them.

"They are," Kelvin said, "and they know Sarah's writing a story about it too. Pretty sure they've already signed off on that, isn't that right?"

"It is," said Sarah.

Fifteen minutes later, Kelvin was sitting on a broad stage in front of the senior care's dining room. Vanessa, her two boys, Sarah, and Livvie sat off to one side. Promptly at five, Kelvin launched into a performance of "Down by the Riverside," followed by "Where Have All the Flowers Gone," "Fly Me to the Moon," and "All You Need Is Love."

Each song was applauded, and many of the residents sang along. Several women waved their hands in the air to the music, and one stood up and danced in a circle.

Vanessa watched her sons. Drew jumped up and down during the more upbeat songs, and Buster seemed engaged. He wasn't his usual distant, silent self, but made crooning noises, some of which seemed to Vanessa even to be on key. He rubbed his arms, but not as though he was in pain; this was a more self-soothing mode of touch. Vanessa was certain the concert was a positive, perhaps even invigorating, experience for him, and she was determined to expose him to more music whenever she could.

Sarah saw that Livvie was at ease during the performance. Instead of attempting to writhe away from her mother's arms, Livvie was quiet and appeared to be listening, though Sarah couldn't be sure.

Sarah was inspired to see so many seniors, who walked with the aid of canes or walkers or were brought into the room in wheelchairs, moving to the music, singing along, smiling, and laughing.

She saw the positive effects of music on people of every age and level of ability, and she was grateful that Kelvin so generously invited them to attend his performance.

• • •

Mallard and Ganderson stood in the lab and watched as Richards, the lead crime scene tech, removed two small beige packets from an envelope and, using tweezers, extracted light-brown hairs from each and laid them side by side in a glass dish. He was dressed in a lab coat and wore goggles and purple plastic gloves.

"Know what these are?" Richards asked, a note of pride in his voice.

"Matched hairs?" Ganderson answered.

Richards nodded. "These, on the left, are from the Virginia Rabelson murder scene, and those on the right are from the Lonny Dubon site." He gently put the hairs into their respective packets. "The hair from the Rabelson site was found on the cloth that had been stuffed into Rabelson's mouth. Another was found near her body, just inside the doorway. The hairs from the Dubon site were found on the front of Dubon's shirt, I believe."

"Don't you need the hair roots to do a DNA analysis?" Ganderson asked.

Richards shook his head. "That used to be true, but not anymore. We can use mitochondrial DNA from the hair shaft for identification purposes."

"Have the hairs been run through the system?" Mallard asked; he knew the answer. They wouldn't have been called to the forensic lab unless a match had been found.

Richards nodded and tapped his COVID-19 mask, looking at Ganderson. The latter hated wearing a mask; he considered it a personal affront, an attack on his freedom, so he often skirted the issue by pulling his mask down below his nose—his little protest. Richards was calling him on this. Ganderson raised the mask.

"They're both matches for one Diana Moran—a particularly nasty piece of work, last pulled in for attempted murder. Took four guys to subdue her, two of whom suffered broken arms, another a broken jaw. Tough as they come. She beat the attempted murder rap but has done time for assault and battery—twice. High-level muscle." Richards grinned. "Now she's looking at two murders, once we find her. Pretty sure the DA will approve a plea to some kind of manslaughter if she testifies against her boss."

"Maverick Lockhart," Mallard said.

Richards widened his eyes in affirmation, then touched his mask again. "Mask, Paul."

Ganderson's mask had come down; rather than adjust the mask as requested, Ganderson turned and left the lab. Mallard followed.

"Azaleas," Mallard was saying.

"What?" Ganderson asked.

"And rhododendrons. Just before we went down to the lab, Kay called, and we had a nice chat about plants she's going to have the gardener order for around the front door. Those were his suggestions, and Kay relayed them to me—azaleas and rhododendrons."

"So, you and Kay had a real conversation," Ganderson said, impressed, as they returned to their desks.

Mallard smiled, proud of the accomplishment. "We did, and we got something done. Flowers are good!"

Ganderson looked at his watch. "So, nearly two o'clock, and she hadn't had her first drink for the day. Do you believe her? You sure that gardener isn't planting more than flowers?" He smirked, but Mallard didn't think that was funny at all.

"Who said she didn't have her first drink?"

An alert appeared on Ganderson's screen, and as he opened the file and read its contents, a slow smile spread across his face. "Looks like we have a handle on the source of the incoming firearms."

Mallard looked at his screen and saw the information. "The question is, Do we bring him in?"

• • •

Maverick Lockhart sat behind the desk in his office. Despite the choice of seats in the room, Diana Moran chose to stand to one side of Lockhart's desk, keeping the door in sight. The habit was one of many self-defense behaviors that were second nature to her.

"At this point, let's just keep an eye on them both," Lockhart was saying, "with the focus being on Ellison—she's the lead—if they separate. Basically what you did with Dubon. Shadow her, keep track of her movements, who she sees, where she goes." Lockhart sat back, folded his hands behind his head, and looked at her, his weapon of choice.

Moran nodded but didn't speak. Even when she stood still, she was a coiled predator, ready to spring. She was one of very few people who made the normally supremely confident Lockhart uneasy. It wasn't so much that she could easily kill him at any moment—very likely without breaking a sweat—but the possibility that she might, in fact, choose to do so. She was a loose cannon—a valuable one—but a loose cannon nonetheless. She had a tendency to go rogue and leave a mess behind—and she never cleaned up after herself. To Moran, brutalizing people was fun. She would have to be eliminated, but not yet. She was still of use. She was one of the few aces he held against Ellison, who was, with the help of her partner, Winters, wily, smart, and formidable.

He watched her as he would watch a particularly venomous snake. "What you did with Lonny, giving his description to the cops as a red herring," he said as he jabbed his finger several times in her direction. "That was smart." He was stroking her out of anxiety, hoping to whisper her, sedate her with compliments. "So was your idea to affect that NIMBY stance around Montgomery and to keep an apartment in the vicinity."

She didn't react to the compliment, but looked at him much as a snake might at a future meal. "Only a block from my real place, and anyone who's weak disgusts me."

Out of nervousness, he went on. "Far as taking out Lonny—plausible deniability is always a good thing. Sometimes the best way to save the body is to cut off an arm."

Moran smiled her crocodile smile, showing holes where some of her teeth should have been; it was an unnerving smile because it was so out of place on her macabre visage.

"Enough of freaking your wife out. Gonna let me at her? How 'bout it? Open the fuckin' gate."

Lockhart considered the request; he'd been obsessed with his ex since she'd become his ex, since she'd been with that damn lawyer, Bishop, which she'd probably done with an eye toward divorce. Bishop was supposedly a good lawyer. Maverick idly wondered if he did divorces and if he could handle a girlfriend's divorce. He was surprised not to have received papers yet. Moran understood his need to squeeze the joy, any joy, from Emily's life. His need was more than a desire—it was a biological imperative. When he couldn't pull Emily back to him, he'd made it his life's mission to make her pay, to make her miserable, to make her see that without him, she was nothing. Without him, she would be forever miserable.

He'd done that and more. But still, it wasn't enough. Well, Moran was right. It was time. Emily had to go. He'd taken away her most valued treasure—her son. He'd wrung what misery he could from her soul, and now she and her lawyer friend would have to die.

• • •

Dora had been lying on the bed, twirling multiple strands of her hair around the forefinger of her left hand, then yanking them out and laying them on the sheet next to her head. She was in a trance-like state, not thinking while she did this.

She noticed Missy in the doorway. She may have been there for some time, but to Dora, she appeared there just then. Dora shifted her gaze to Missy and moved her hand to her side.

"Why would Maverick Lockhart have hired us if he was behind his own son's murder?" Missy asked. "It doesn't make sense on any level."

Dora sat up and self-consciously touched her finger to the back of her head. When it came away with blood, she wiped it on her pants and stood up. She could tell when Missy had something specific in mind. "It could be an ingenious take on returning to the scene of the crime—and he could keep tabs on any investigation."

Missy shook her head. "But he's creating the investigation."

"A kid's murdered, there's going to be an investigation no matter what."

"But he isn't keeping tabs on the cops," Missy said.

"He probably figures we're as good as they are. What we know, and share with him, they probably know."

Missy said, "I suggest we pay Maverick a visit, tell him about the progress we've made and see if my profiling studies have taught me anything."

"Profiling studies?" Dora repeated, not understanding.

Missy nodded eagerly. "I've found several books on profiling and watched a few tutorials. I'd like to try out some of what I've learned on Maverick Lockhart." She began taking off her clothes, then went into the bathroom. "I'll be in the shower," she said. "Do you want to call Lockhart to see when we can come by?"

"Okay. I'm sure he's chomping at the bit for a report." Dora got up, went to the dining room table, wincing at the pain on the side of her mouth and her ribs. She opened a report she'd received from Lieutenant Catherine Trask. The report had been sent in exchange for her own report. Dora scanned the file a second time, while her mind wandered over recent events. She'd been replaying in her mind her clash with the skeletal woman, looking for what she could have done differently. The woman was a preternatural striker and submission artist—world-class, and without any inhibitions against deadly force.

Dora thought she saw a glimmer of possibility, an avenue of technique she herself had experienced recently—technique that, in another arena, had nullified her own striking and submission prowess. Perhaps she might put it to use, should the opportunity arise.

"Did you talk to Lockhart?" Missy was standing in the entrance to the hallway that led to the bathroom and bedroom, naked and drying her hair with a blue towel.

"I'll do that now." Dora took out her phone and pressed Lockhart's number. "This is Dora Ellison calling for Maverick Lockhart," she said to the receptionist. "He'll know what it's about."

After a moment, Lockhart's voice said, "Dora, what do you have?"

"Can Missy and I come by? We'd prefer to present our information in person."

"I feel the same. The sooner the better."

"Give us half an hour."

"Done."

Chapter 24

Sarah found a children's musical on YouTube and was streaming it to the TV in her living room. She had Livvie in her lap, had grasped her daughter's little arms between her fingers and thumbs, and was waving them in time to the music. Vanessa was doing much the same with Buster. Of the two, Livvie seemed the more engaged, though Buster was a year and a half older. Drew was dancing in place in front of the TV, bending from side to side to the beat of the music and flailing his arms. Drew loved music and had bonded with Kelvin, who sat cross-legged on the floor, next to Vanessa, drumming his palms on his knees, his shoulder occasionally brushing Vanessa's. While he was facing the TV, his attention was on Vanessa and her boys, and hers was on him. Her smile was easy and unaffected, as though a weight of sadness and fear had been lifted from her and she was better able to enjoy the moment. Kelvin had helped loosen and flush her terror from her.

"You know," he said, "my work at Montgomery and my performances for seniors aren't full-time. You work nights, right?"

Vanessa nodded.

"Who watches the boys when you're at work?"

She blew out a breath. "Whew! It's challenging! Friends—Shanice James, Nia Paulson, Dora Ellison … Whoever's available."

"Maybe I can help."

Vanessa's eyes widened with hope. Sarah, still sitting nearby with Livvie, overheard and leaned in, listening.

"I can make time a few evenings a week," Kelvin offered. "And I could do some music therapy with both boys—mostly Buster."

"Could you? Would you?" Her eyes were tearing.

Kelvin touched Vanessa's arm, and Vanessa leaned over and hugged him.

"That would mean so much," she said. "You're giving me hope." The tears overflowed, spilling down her face.

Sarah was watching, her eyebrows raised. "I don't suppose you have any time during the day. I work on *The Chronicle* all day, and I have Livvie here, and it's gotten to be a bit much."

Kelvin thought about this. "I could probably give you three or four hours a couple times a week if I move some things around."

"And it wouldn't inconvenience you or anybody?" Sarah asked.

Kelvin laughed. "Not your problem."

"Really?" Sarah glanced at Vanessa. "And it wouldn't take away from 'Nessa's boys?"

Kelvin shook his head. "Nah."

The apartment door opened, and C3 came in, stopping when he saw the crowd in his living room. "Hey," he said, forcing a smile.

Sarah could see he was upset. He was blinking, something he did when he was overwhelmed or sad.

"Listen, guys," Sarah said. "I have some work stuff I have to take care of. Can we catch up tomorrow?" She reached out and took Kelvin's hand. "And thank you." She shook her head. "Either way. Maybe we can talk about a schedule."

"Absolutely," Kelvin replied.

"C'mon, Drew." Vanessa stood up, but Drew was dancing with the TV. She took a few moments to belt Buster into his car seat, then put the boys' toys into her travel bag, which she slung over her shoulder. She picked up the seat with Buster in it. "Drew—time to go home."

Drew continued dancing, his little hips gyrating from front to back and side to side.

"Sarah?" Vanessa said, nodding toward the TV.

Sarah got the message and turned the TV off, and Drew looked at her in disbelief. Sarah laughed at the seriousness of his expression.

"C'mon, Drew," Vanessa said, all business now as she stepped toward the door. "Buster and I are going. Are you coming?"

Not wanting to be left behind, Drew ran for his mother's outstretched hand. "Don't forget me!" he cried, then stopped in the doorway. "Kelvin go too!" he cried.

"No, Drew. Kelvin's staying here, but we'll see Kelvin later, and you can sing with him then, okay?"

"Nooo!" Drew wailed, then thought for a moment, a finger in his mouth. "Singing with Kelvin a surprise for Mommy," he explained, so seriously than Vanessa laughed out loud, then covered her mouth and looked at Kelvin. She glanced quickly at then away from Kelvin, and spoke softly to Drew until he forgot about Kelvin and about the singing and went willingly with his mother.

Once Vanessa and her boys had left, Sarah put her arms around C3 and held him. She could feel the grief pouring from him—a weight dragging him down emotionally so that he wasn't able to return her hug.

"Billy?" she asked.

He didn't answer. He didn't have to.

They stood in one another's arms for some time before C3 said, "My father wants us to come by."

"What for?" Sarah asked.

C3 shrugged, but the way he refused to meet her eye gave Sarah a clue that he knew what was going on.

Sarah looked at Kelvin. "Stay with Livvie?"

Kelvin nodded and grinned. "Sure!"

Sarah rolled her eyes at C3. "Does everyone know what's going on here but me?"

Kelvin looked baffled and shrugged. "Don't know what you mean."

• • •

Sarah and C3 arrived at Charlie and Christine's apartment and spent the first several minutes admiring Christine's baby bump, which she'd dressed to emphasize in a floor-length gray V-neck sheath dress. She was radiant, and she claimed that her and baby's health were "just perfect." Charlie, too, was exuberant and babbled about his ideas for decorating the baby's room and his thoughts for the first few months after the baby's birth, when Christine would take a leave of absence from City Hall and Charlie would lean on Vanessa to shoulder some of the burden at The Bernelli Group.

Christine and Charlie sat next to one another on one side of the double-crescent sunken couch, Charlie's arm casually around his wife's shoulders on the sofa back.

C3 and Sarah sat across from them. Everyone drank soda, and if Charlie was uncomfortable with the enforced alcohol-free environment, he didn't show it.

"So, I understand things aren't going so well with LaChance," Charlie began, looking at Sarah.

Sarah whirled to glare at C3, who looked sheepish. She turned back to Charlie. "Actually, the paper's running fine. Let's just say LaChance likes to, um, stir the pot."

"She's being polite, Pop," C3 interjected, to another glare from Sarah. "He's got people writing letters and posting on social media about people with special needs being less-than-worthwhile members of society."

"The social media part's got nothing to do with *The Chronicle*," Sarah said.

"But he's fomenting this stuff," Charlie pointed out. "Look, I know LaChance. This conflict's got him all over it. I thought it would be good for *The Chronicle*'s bottom line."

"And it has been," Sarah admitted.

"But at what expense?" Charlie continued. No one answered. "Right. Well, I know you take pride in your work—you have an admirable degree of journalistic integrity."

"She does," Christine added, looking pointedly at Sarah. "We love that about you—and I'm speaking as the mayor as much as your de facto mother-in-law." She shrugged. "I suppose I'm also speaking as a Christian."

"My understanding," Charlie said, clearing his throat, "is that you'd just as soon be rid of LaChance."

"There's no point in discussing that, Charlie," Sarah said dismissively. "We owe him the money he's laid out, with interest."

Charlie held up a finger. "Yes, Sarah, you do. But what if he was paid off and you were left with a loan you could pay at your leisure, no interest, and—hear me now—with 100 percent journalistic license."

"Who would— You?" Sarah was aghast. "No! No! I couldn't allow you to—"

"Honey," C3 said, his hand over hers. He took her hand in both of his and brought it to his lips. "Honey, I think what you mean to say is, 'thank you, Dad.'"

"You're welcome," Charlie replied, grinning. "Now, let's get on over to the dining room. You too, Chris," he said to Christine. "Your days of serving are over."

Delighted, Christine smiled. "We're having shrimp with mascarpone in cream sauce."

Sarah's reluctance was fading fast. "You made risotto for us to talk about *The Chronicle?*" She was incredulous.

Charlie leaned toward her and whispered, sotto voce, "We ordered out." Christine glared; Charlie shrugged and grinned.

• • •

They met in an upscale yet spartan living room that abutted Maverick Lockhart's office. Dora and Missy sat on a couch that faced Lockhart, who sat in an overstuffed armchair, legs apart, feet on the floor, a confident smile on his face. He leaned forward, rubbing his palms together.

"So, what've you got?" he asked.

Missy had brought a laptop, which was open and on her lap. Dora sat beside her, content to let her take the lead. This was very much Missy's show.

"First of all, I'm going to be referring directly to your son's murder. Please forgive me for that."

Lockhart nodded eagerly, raising his glasses with a thumb and forefinger and looking at Missy from beneath them. "Please proceed."

Missy nodded and pressed her lips together, concentrating. "Well, we've been seeing reports on social media and in letters to the newspaper referring to people with special needs as being less than the rest of us, not deserving care, not being full members of society. To our eyes, this is almost a coordinated campaign of sorts."

Lockhart shrugged. "Not sure what this has to do with my son's murder, but I sympathize. I sometimes wonder about the value handicapped people have—what they can contribute, and I realize that honestly, it isn't much. So I get it."

"Okay," said Missy. "And in line with that, we've learned that people with firearms have been arrested in the vicinity, even on the grounds, of Montgomery."

Dora nodded. "One with a handgun, another with a rifle."

Lockhart squinted, his forehead wrinkled. "Are you saying my son may have been killed by someone who was intentionally targeting disabled people?"

"Perhaps," Missy said, noncommittally, then looked up at Lockhart, who'd replaced his glasses in their original position on his nose. "Some people in the Montgomery community are angry with Montgomery himself."

"That's right," Dora added. "People love the place. Their children and loved ones do well there."

"As did Julian." Lockhart agreed. "You just had to see him and hear him sing to understand."

"Did you see him much?" Dora asked.

Lockhart shrugged. "Now and then."

Dora was careful not to look at Missy. "Montgomery had guaranteed to keep the place going, in perpetuity," she said. "He promised to leave money in his will for his facility to continue, ongoing."

"But he reneged," Missy said. "He changed his mind, and people were angry. And not just a few. Several groups on Facebook were devoted to people's anger at Montgomery."

"Terrible," Lockhart said, shaking his head in solidarity with Missy's words.

"Possibly the angriest of these people was none other than your ex's father—Jack Ashford."

"Son of a bitch!" Lockhart snapped. His feet curled around the legs of his chair, gripping them.

"What's your thought about that?" Missy asked. "Do you think Jack Ashford killed his own grandson—your son?"

Lockhart shifted in his seat so that he was now sitting on his left hip, his torso and face pointed toward the door. He stroked his chin thoughtfully. "I think it's entirely possible—quite likely, in fact—that whoever the shooter was, he was aiming at Montgomery—and may have been working for Ashford." He shook his head, marveling. "I've got to say, you've done a great job."

"We're not done," Missy said.

"You're not?"

"Oh, no."

"Did you know that Jack Ashford has a sniper's rifle?" Dora asked.

Lockhart's eyes widened. "I had no idea!"

"Now, you might wonder who Ashford's accomplice was." Missy watched Lockhart carefully.

Lockhart put a palm to his forehead, a thumb and middle finger briefly rubbing his temples. "You know?" His voice had dropped to barely more than a whisper.

"A man named Richard Dubon, nickname of Lonny," Missy explained.

Lockhart touched his hand to his neck, stroking it several times, listening. He picked a piece of lint from the sleeve of his shirt. He blew air out his lips, puffing his cheeks. "What do you know about this guy?"

"We've learned a bit," Dora said, cryptically. "He's dead, for one thing. Brutally murdered."

Lockhart clamped his thighs with both hands, rubbing them forward and back. "Well, you've done an exemplary job. Let me cut you a check for the full amount. I believe I have your invoice on my desk." He left the room and returned a moment later with the Geller Investigations invoice and his checkbook in one hand, the other hand thrust into his pants pocket with a thumb and the fingers hanging outside the pocket.

He laid the invoice and checkbook side by side—the invoice on the right, since he wrote with his left hand. His legs curled again around the legs of his chair.

"Why don't you make it out for half," Dora suggested. "After all, this isn't definitive."

"I'd say it's pretty damned good!"

"We're working on information that's more definitive, concerning your wife."

Lockhart's face darkened, his legs uncurled again from the chair, and he thrust his face forward. Then, just as quickly, his features relaxed and his expression calmed. "Ex-wife—though technically we're still married, and I'm glad you brought her up. I'd love to talk to her. While we disagree on much, we've lost the one thing we had in common—our son. I'd like to offer her condolences and find a way to coexist, if not get along."

Dora smiled. "That's nice to hear. We'll let you know what we learn."

"As far as I know, she's disappeared." Lockhart said, both arms out, palms up. "I haven't been able to find her. As far as I'm concerned, finding her is another job for you, and I insist on paying for it separately."

"Well, let's wait until we get you that information," Missy said.

"And we will," Dora assured him. "We'll find out where she is and when, and with whom."

"Find her lawyer boyfriend as well, if you can."

Dora smiled. "We'll see what we can do."

Maverick Lockhart sat back, his knee up in front of him, using it as a table on which to set the checkbook as he wrote the check. He tore it off and handed it to Missy.

"Nice job, ladies."

Chapter 25

Back at the apartment, Dora sat down on the floor, and Freedom came over and laid her head in her lap. Dora watched as Missy put on a Bach playlist—soothing-yet-structured music that calmed her and gently reorganized her mind.

Missy then sat down behind Dora, pulled her head back into her lap, and began massaging her temples.

"How are you, Dor? Feeling better?"

"Keep doing that. I'm fine."

"Uh-huh."

"Really."

"It's okay to be not fine, Dor."

"Just keep doing that. It feels good."

"Want to hear how the profiling went?" Missy sounded excited.

"You learned something from it?" Dora asked.

"I'm a librarian."

Dora laughed.

"First of all, it's hard to spot deception. It's not as simple as a person looking down or to the left or something like that."

"You can rub my head while you're talking, you know."

"Yup. So Lockhart started by leaning forward and rubbing his hands together—a position of happy excitement. Engagement."

"I remember," Dora said."

"When I brought up the social media posts about people with special needs being less-than-equal citizens, he not only didn't react negatively, which you'd expect of most reasonably compassionate people, but he said he understood that viewpoint. Red flag."

"And his own son has special needs!"

"Had," Missy corrected her.

"Right."

"Then, when I first mentioned Julian's murder, he squinted, which is classic eye-blocking. A sign of nervousness, but understandable, given the subject. But also a possible sign of anxiety about a crime he could be involved with."

"Fair enough."

"Then, when I mentioned Jack Ashford being angry, he curled his legs around the armchair's legs, rooting himself in place—an expression of anxiety, of needing to feel more anchored."

"Huh. Interesting."

Missy was excited to explain everything she'd noticed about Lockhart and the signs she'd seen in his behavior. "When we asked about the possibility that Ashford killed his grandson, Lockhart's son, he angled his body away and pointed his feet toward the door—a sign of wanting to escape."

"And pretty obvious, the way you describe it."

"Though that might just indicate his disagreement with the concept."

"Oh, okay."

"Profiling isn't so cut and dried. It's more a cumulative coalescing of information. How does it all add up? Anyway, he also wanted to end the conversation right there and pay us, saying we'd done a great job."

"He did," Dora said, nodding.

"We then talked about how Jack Ashford owns a sniper rifle but had been on the stage just after Julian had been shot, so he had to have an accomplice—Lonny Dubon—who worked for Maverick, and who we all know was just murdered. As soon as we mentioned him, Lockhart put a thumb and finger to his temples, another anxiety movement, and when we mentioned Dubon by name, he stroked his neck, a pacifying behavior. We were making him very nervous by talking about Dubon. He was trying to end the conversation. He also picked lint from his shirt and blew air out his lips—more anxiety. Here again, he wanted to end the conversation, and then he rubbed his thighs, signifying his desire to escape."

"Wow."

Missy held up a "but wait" finger. "But here's the kicker—the conversation turned to Emily, and he changed. He became, however briefly, angry and aggressive, and his feet left the protective legs of the chair and sat flat on the floor in a wide, more confident stance."

"Amazing you picked all this up."

Missy shrugged. "I'm a librarian. I research. I learn. But then, when he wrote us the check, he did so using his knee as a table. He put his leg between us, shielding himself. More anxiety, and a need for self-protection. On some level, I think we're freaking him out. He wants to get rid of us. Pay us and be done."

Dora sat up, moving Freedom away, turned, and kissed Missy on the mouth. "You're a genius. No, I know—a librarian."

"Same thing," Missy said, giggling. She gave Dora three quick kisses.

Dora held Missy at arm's length, inclining her head and steadily holding her gaze. "Do you agree that Maverick Lockhart's body language confirms Emily's accusation—that he had his son killed to get at her?"

• • •

The Forestville Inn was an immense white Victorian estate in Lake George, New York, that had been turned into an inn ninety-five years earlier. Its wrap-around porch, sporting nearly a dozen green wooden rocking chairs, faced the main road. Opposite the inn, glittering in the late-summer sun, was the lake—with multiple docks for rentable paddleboats, parasailing, a nearby local railroad, wineries, museums, fishing, and tours of the vicinity.

Emily and her boyfriend, the lawyer Robert Bishop, were booked in one suite at the inn, Dora and Missy in another. The two couples were sitting in the living room of Emily and Robert's suite, discussing the plan Dora and Missy had laid out for capturing Maverick Lockhart and his assassin. The plan's foundation had been Emily's idea.

"Why are you so sure Maverick will believe that you want to meet?" Missy asked.

"I've known Maverick a long time," Emily said, and glanced at Robert, who was seated on the bed next to her, holding her hand. "He's so self-centered that he thinks of others only as they relate to him. If he's told I want to offer him condolences, he'll think it's only natural because he's the center of the universe. Everything should be about him. Everyone should come to him. He has real blinders in that sense."

"Well, your lives are at risk, so you'd better be right."

"Oh, I am," Emily said confidently.

"There's something I've been wondering," Missy said to Emily. "Why didn't you tell us before that you thought Maverick killed Julian?"

Emily took a deep breath and exhaled through pursed lips. "Because I'm terrified of Maverick." She blinked a few times. "I just didn't want to open that door. I didn't want to go there. I didn't want to put it out there. He hadn't killed me yet. Maybe accusing him, even in private, would be that last straw…"

"Fair enough," Dora said. She shifted gears. "Missy texted him your suite and elicited his guarantee that he wouldn't share it with anyone. We suspect that he and his assassin will attempt to gain access to your suite with some simple ruse—a delivery, an offer of extra towels, or some complimentary concierge-related service, such as information about local activities you might like."

Missy glanced at Dora before Dora continued. "We expect that you'll be accosted and probably attacked by Diana Moran, a thin woman with light-brown hair. She's extremely violent and dangerous."

"She's a killer who, as far as we know, works exclusively for Lockhart," Missy added.

"Well, Maverick's violent too," Emily added. "Don't sell him short in that area."

"Maybe," Dora said. "But Diana Moran is the tool he uses to express his violence. She looks like a skinny, kind of trashy, woman, but she's a trained killer, so treat her as such."

"I have some questions," Robert said, his mouth a thin line of concern. "Have the police been alerted, and do they have the proof they need to arrest and prosecute?" Worry creases appeared in his forehead.

Dora and Missy looked at one another. Missy spoke. "The police will be alerted. The issue for us will be timing. We want to catch Lockhart and Moran in the act without scaring them away. And we need to discuss how we'll go about gathering the evidence the police will need."

"To that end," Dora continued, "you'll be bait, but we'll see to it that you're safe at all times."

"I hope so," Bishop said, settling his enormous black-rimmed glasses on his nose. The mixture of hope and concern in his eyes was magnified by the thick lenses. He stroked Emily's hand with his thumb. "While the inn and surrounding area are gorgeous, we're not going to be able to enjoy any of it until these people are behind bars."

Emily leaned over and kissed him. "Long as I'm with you, how bad can it be?" She was smiling, but her voice was unsteady and anxious.

Bishop smiled, then looked at Dora, his expression suddenly serious. "Is there anything we need to do, or say, or set up in advance of whatever you have planned?"

Dora was clenching and unclenching a fist. "I'm glad you asked. Here's a list of what each of us needs to do."

• • •

Emily lay back on the bed, with Bishop on top of her. He'd removed his glasses and begun kissing her, his fingers fumbling with the buttons on her blouse.

Emily held up a hand. "I thought you said you couldn't enjoy any of this until Maverick's behind bars."

Bishop smiled. "What I meant was, I can't enjoy the attractions of the area. But you, you I can enjoy anywhere, anytime." He kissed her neck, and she held him to her with a gentle hand on the back of his head.

He sensed her anxiety and sat up. "I trust Dora. I've known her for a while, and I'm sure she knows what she's doing."

She swallowed, and he could see how frightened she was. He pulled her into a hug. "Shhh. We'll be okay."

She moaned with fear. "I'm on pins and needles." She startled at a soft knock on the door and rebuttoned her blouse. "Just a minute." She nodded to Bishop, who went to the door. His own shirt was unbuttoned and hung loosely over his pants. He looked through the peephole, then opened the door.

"It's Dora. She's alone."

Bishop opened the door and let Dora into the room.

"Okay, guys. Here's how we're going to do this."

• • •

Forty minutes later there came two light knocks on the door.

"Yes?" Bishop asked.

"Complimentary flowers and champagne," came a woman's sunny response.

Dora frowned. The cheerful voice didn't jibe with her memory of Diana Moran, so she peered through the peephole. If circumstances had been different, she might have laughed. The woman was indeed Diana

Moran, but she wore a bright-yellow apron, a yellow blouse, and a blue name tag with the logo and name of a floral delivery company. The smile on her face looked false and out of place. In her hands were a vase and a gift-wrapped item in the shape of a bottle.

Bishop glanced at Dora, who nodded. He opened the door and stepped back into the room.

Instantly, several things happened nearly simultaneously.

With Dora behind the door, Bishop had stepped back to give Moran space to step into the room. With a suspicious glance toward Dora, as though she could see through the door, Moran took a step to her left and away from the door, but not quite far enough away. Dora threw her weight against the heavy security door, slamming it against Moran's right arm, which was cradled against her, holding the vase to her body. The tall, sleek glass vase was knocked against Moran's cheek, and it crashed to the floor, shattering and revealing a small pink handgun in Moran's hand.

Robert Bishop had herded Emily into the bathroom and Moran's eyes followed them. She was about to speak when Dora, who was still clasping the knob on the other side of the door, pulled back and slammed the door several times against Moran's arm until the gun clattered to the floor and Moran was thrown off-balance to her left. She quickly righted herself and saw Dora, then a smile spread across her face.

"Hey there, cookie." She looked delighted.

Dora said nothing but leaped at the woman's feet, taking her by surprise and dragging her to the floor. Dora pressed herself against her adversary, never giving her room to operate, but Moran managed to wriggle away and struggle to her feet. She threw two quick, sharp punches, hitting Dora in the nose, which splattered open, spurting blood into the carpet. The blood seemed to excite Moran, and when Dora threw a left hook, Moran caught and held Dora's fist with her right hand and attempted a submission. But Dora pulled away, then sprang forward again, taking Moran by surprise and throwing an elbow and knee as she did so. The knee caught Moran, who'd initially been pulled toward Dora, on the cheek, breaking her face open. Now blood from the two women sprayed them both and leaked to the floor.

Dora jumped to her feet and looked around for Missy but didn't see her. Moran was also on her feet, and the two women faced off, Moran in a conventional stance, Dora in a reverse, southpaw, stance. For a moment, nothing happened. Then, the women threw simultaneous lead punches—Moran a left and Dora a right. Because Dora was the bigger of the two women, hers was the punch that landed. Dora continued to push forward and extend her arms around the slighter woman. Her arms encircled Moran's chest and clasped behind her back. Dora pressed forward, shifted her weight quickly to one side, and twisted Moran to the ground. Dora was on top and attempting to posture up to rain blows down upon her opponent, but Moran had locked her arms around Dora's chest and back and was pulling Dora down and holding her close against her.

Dora managed to press herself up and away and punch Moran several times in the face, creating some space between them. She quickly rained a vicious left and then a right down on Moran's face and could feel the air leave Moran's lungs. She stayed as close as she could on top of Moran, refusing to give the assassin space to maneuver and pulling back only for a moment to allow herself room to bash the woman in the face and neck.

Moran tried several up-elbows, but Dora buried her face in the crook of her own left elbow and slammed first her forehead and then her torso down as hard as she could onto Moran's chest. Very few blows could match a headbutt for raw power. Dora felt some of the strength leave her opponent, so she slipped her left arm around Moran's back, holding their two bodies close against one another. With both arms in position and Moran's arms trapped, Dora began to squeeze.

Moran bucked and pushed, trying to gain a foothold against Dora's hips. Dora moved and slid but held her position. Moran twisted, but Dora refused to give an inch. She had Moran exactly where she wanted her. Dora kept squeezing, then pressed her weight forward and squeezed some more. Moran flailed helplessly, took one deep breath, and tried to writhe away, then lay still.

Dora continued squeezing. After a few more minutes, she relaxed her grip. Moran's head flopped to the side; she was unconscious.

"Well, that was fun," Maverick Lockhart was in the half-open doorway, standing next to a short, freckled, intense-looking man with a Beretta M9 in his hand. The two men stepped into the room and quickly moved several feet apart.

Dora smiled and shook her head. "Always need someone else to fight your battles. Who's your pal?"

Lockhart laughed. "His name's Bannion, and my battles *are* his battles."

Robert Bishop had ventured out of the bathroom and was staring at Bannion. "You're who's responsible for the influx of guns. They're coming in through your shop."

Bannion was still—too still. The corner of his mouth twitched. "And?"

"Where's Emily?" Lockhart demanded. "Emily," he called. "Come on out, or I blow a hole in your boyfriend's face."

The bathroom door opened, and Emily stepped gingerly into the room.

"That's a good girl."

"Lockhart," Dora said, "I get why you want to hurt your wife, but what do you have against your own son?"

"I never had anything against him," Lockhart responded. "I couldn't have cared less about him one way or another. But when I learned that my wife was cheating on me ..." He shrugged. He turned to Emily. "I never really loved you anyway."

Emily's eyes widened, and her eyebrows arched. "Well, I loved *you*. We were soulmates, and you know it. I said so, and you said so. We were in love, Maverick. And it was true love!"

Maverick Lockhart's gaze wavered. He blinked. "Well then, what the fuck did you cheat on me for?"

Furious, Emily was breathing heavily. "Because I misjudged you. I thought you cared about me. I thought you cared about your son!"

Lockhart laughed. "Get your story straight. You just said I loved you, then you said you misjudged me. Which is it?"

"Both. You did love me, to the degree you're capable of love, I guess. But whatever love you had for me paled next to the love you had for yourself. And you never cared about your son!" Her expression turned fierce. "You killed our son, you piece of shit!"

Lockhart shrugged again. "You had to be taught a lesson, by some means that would get through, that would send a message." He grinned. "And that would really, really hurt."

"So you killed an innocent young man, a brilliantly talented young man—and your own son!"

"I did. And I'd say it worked, don't you think? You're pretty devastated." He smiled at Emily, who cringed away. "I was going to put it all on your father—on poor old Jack, who really did love his grandson, so much so that he desperately wanted to spare him life in an institution. I would have thought people would believe that, wouldn't you think? Killing his grandson to keep him out of the cruel, cruel system?"

He smiled. "And Mason Montgomery added an intriguing ingredient. He reneged on his promise to keep his school going—pissing off a lot of people, including Jack—and voilà, there was another possibility. Maybe Jack had to kill Montgomery for reneging on his promise to keep that place going. Only," he said with a shrug, "what a shame Jack missed and hit his grandson, killing him."

"You're one sick fuck,," Emily groaned.

"Maybe so, but I won, didn't I? I've got my revenge, and my man Bannion here has the gun." Lockhart looked from Dora to Emily with a satisfied smirk. "And let me tell you something about Julian. Yeah, he was my son, but I'm ashamed to have fathered a defective kid. And you can't tell me he was anything else. I despise anyone who's weak, and there's no one weaker than one of these crippled kids. Tell you what—

I'd be thrilled to never see one of your so-called special people again."
He shook his head, disgusted. "Special kids," he muttered.

"Time to drop the gun, Bannion," said a voice. Missy was standing in the doorway, feet apart, both hands around the stock of Diana Moran's small, pink Springfield XD-S, which she'd picked up from the floor only moments before. She pulled her phone from the pocket of her flannel shirt. "Everything 'til now was recorded." She waggled her eyebrows at Lockhart. "Librarians are big on facts—like evidence."

Dora grinned at Bannion and Lockhart. "Here's what you're going to do. Missy's going to walk Bannion outside, where the police are either waiting or about to arrive. I'll stay here and keep Lockhart company."

Lockhart's eyes darted from Missy to Bannion to Dora, then back to Bannion. "Don't listen to her, Tommy."

Bannion swiveled toward Missy, who grimaced and quickly fired off a shot. "Shit!" he yelled. Blood spurted from Bannion's right forearm, forcing him to drop the gun, reach for the wound, and cry out.

Missy nodded toward the door. "Outside, Bannion."

The gun shop and range owner did as he was told.

Missy followed Bannion out into the hotel hallway, and the door to the room swung closed.

Bannion's face was clenched against the pain, and he was doubled over, clutching his arm. "Can I get some medical attention?" He was breathing heavily through his nose.

"Nope," Missy said, taking a few steps away but keeping the pistol aimed at his midsection. "We wait."

Chapter 26

Inside the hotel room, Lockhart backed away from Dora. "What are you going to do?" he asked, his voice shaking.

"I'm going to make your wish come true."

"Wish? What wish?"

"You'll never have to see another person with special needs again."

"What? How—"

• • •

In the hallway, Missy remained several feet from Bannion, the gun pointing steadily at his chest.

Lockhart's voice was screaming from inside the room. "No! For God's sake! No!" Two short screams were followed by one long bellow of agony.

"What the hell is she doing to him?" Bannion lamented.

Missy raised her eyebrows and twisted her mouth ruefully. "Sounds to me like Lockhart's had some sort of accident."

The elevator doors opened, and Mallard, Ganderson, and two uniformed Lake George officers ran into the hallway, guns drawn.

"Hand me the gun, Missy," Ganderson ordered.

Missy did as she was told.

Mallard opened the hotel room door to find Dora bending over Maverick Lockhart, who was unconscious and lying on his side, blood gushing from the area above his nose. A pen with the name of the hotel was on the floor nearby. The pen had blood on its tip, but the rest of it had been wiped clean.

"We found him like this, Bannion and that woman." Dora chinned in the direction of Moran. "Along with him," she said. "I had to subdue the woman. Missy took her gun and held Bannion until you got here. I'm guessing the woman attacked Lockhart, though it's possible Bannion did."

Missy handed Mallard her phone. "Lockhart's confession's on this, but what happened here is not."

Ganderson's fists were on his hips. His mouth twisted, and he blew out a harsh breath. "Why is it that when we find ourselves at a gruesome crime scene, you're always there."

Dora huffed a breath. "If you mean, why do you arrive at crime scenes where somehow justice has been served before you had a chance to intervene, my answer would be 'You're welcome.'"

Ganderson took out a pair of handcuffs and dangled them in front of Dora. "Wrists, please."

Dora had known this was coming; she hoped it wouldn't last long. She proffered her wrists.

Ganderson cuffed her. "I'm arresting you for aggravated assault in the first degree, and possible assault and battery in the second degree." He read her her rights.

Mallard squinted at Missy's phone and turned to her. "We'll need this for a day, perhaps two, at forensics. But you'll get it back."

"No worries," Missy said.

Mallard walked to where Diana Moran lay, knelt beside her, and put a finger to her neck, then rose and looked at his partner. "This woman's deceased."

Ganderson addressed Dora. "So we need to up the latter charge to second degree murder." Dora was about to say something, but Ganderson waved a finger. "We'll let our crime scene people do their job, then we'll get everyone downtown and sort this out. The Lake George PD has generously donated the space and personnel to help us get this done."

• • •

"You've got to be kidding!" It was several hours later, and Ganderson was pacing back and forth in the interview room at the Beach City Police Department headquarters. Mallard was sitting on the edge of the table.

Dora, whose handcuffs had just been removed, was wringing her hands to regain feeling in them.

Her lawyer, Levi Cohen, was a frail, balding man with wire-frame glasses. "What's not to believe, Detective? You've got a couple of killers off the streets, the most horrific murder in years is now solved, and sizable groups of angry families are now mollified."

Ganderson stopped pacing and pointed a finger at the little lawyer. "Except that your client looks to me to be guilty of some pretty brutal violence."

"'Looks to you' isn't proof that will stand up in court, sir. In any case, you have her statement and nothing to contradict her except the word of a world-class gunrunner."

"Alleged!" Ganderson countered.

Levi laughed. "The other statements, while they may not line up perfectly, in no way implicate Ms. Ellison."

"He's got you there, Paulie," Mallard pointed out.

"Who the hell's side are you on?" Ganderson demanded of his partner.

"The side of the law."

Ganderson gave an exasperated sigh. "She claims that the deceased woman mutilated Lockhart—put out his eyes! Except the deceased woman worked for him!"

Mallard shrugged. "You have all sorts of internecine disagreements in the criminal world. You've been privy to quite a few, in fact."

"And I've got one of the most prominent lawyers in town and his girlfriend, who's technically Lockhart's wife, who claim to know nothing about how Lockhart's former employee was killed or who put out Lockhart's eyes. And to top it off, we've got Lockhart himself, who's in a hospital bed, refusing to say anything at all about any of this!"

"All true," Mallard agreed. "Er, ah— Quite the situation, eh, Paulie?"

"So tell me this, Gerry. How did this woman—"

"Moran. Diana Moran."

"Right. How did she manage to put out Lockhart's eyes when she was dead?"

Mallard shrugged, unperturbed, which further infuriated his partner. "Well, obviously she wasn't dead when that occurred. Don't you think, ah, Paulie?"

"Don't I think? Don't I think? Well then, who killed her?"

Mallard had to stop to think. "I believe Ellison claimed that the woman attacked her, and she—what was the expression she used—put her to sleep."

Ganderson gave Mallard a hard look. "She's more than asleep, Gerry."

"I don't think her death was intentional, according to Ellison. She put her in a chokehold to render her unconscious, and the lack of oxygen …" Mallard shrugged. "And Winters's testimony backs this up, more or less."

"Indirectly, but she says no one was in the room except Moran and Ellison!"

"She says that no one was in the room when Moran accosted Ellison, so we can't confirm that Moran died as a result of Ellison's hold. The ME will have to give us that information."

Ganderson threw his hands in the air. "A clusterfuck—that's what this is. A clusterfuck!"

"Look at it this way, Paulie. Er, ah, we have the Julian Lockhart murderer—"

"Alleged murderer!"

Mallard held a hand out, palm down, like a stop sign. "Alleged—for now. But we do have a recorded confession. Anyway, think of all the work-related pressure that came out of that boy's murder. The nonsense in the newspapers and social media about people with disabilities. The uproar from parents and the special-needs community at large. Now that we know who killed the Lockhart kid, all that goes away, or should at least dissipate. And while Ellison might get some of the credit, we'll get some too."

"Ha!" Ganderson made a dismissive gesture. "Thanks only to Cathy Trask's big mouth."

Mallard looked philosophical. "Well, you seem rather fond of Cathy Trask's big mouth."

Ganderson turned a deep shade of red; Mallard continued. "Sometimes it's good to share information. And besides, you'll get credit for stopping the flow of illegal firearms into not only the city but also the county and possibly the state."

That stopped Ganderson, who looked surprised. "Do you think so?"

"Don't you want credit?"

Ganderson shrugged and looked away. "Not a big deal to me."

Epilogue

The auditorium at the Montgomery School was filled with students, parents, families, and friends of the school's attendees. On the stage were the Montgomery Performers, led by Penny Bright, who danced among them and twirled a long silk ribbon while the other performers sang.

When the performance was over, Principal Claire Sumner took the stage. "Weren't they wonderful!" She held out her hands, applauding the troupe, joined by the audience and the performers themselves.

"Today is a special, special day for our people," Sumner said, once the applause had died. "We're so excited to announce the LaChance Williams Special Program at the Montgomery School, named for our new sponsor, Mr. LaChance Williams. Mr. Williams, would you like to say a few words?"

"I would indeed," LaChance replied, as he ascended the stage. After his speech and two more songs, everyone in attendance was invited to the cafeteria for a party.

Kelvin sat at the front of the cafeteria, playing his piano and singing while Vanessa and her boys sat at the first table, enjoying their pizza and fruit drinks. Drew sang some of the songs along with him, while Buster sat on his mother's lap, her hand on his belly, his attention elsewhere.

Most of Montgomery's attendees were in the room, along with nearly as many teachers, aides, and companions.

Penny Bright fluttered between tables, greeting everyone she could name and many she couldn't. "Hello, Robert! Hi, William! Lady, good to see you! Hi, Sean! Hello, Sharleece! Hey, LaChance!"

Her mother, Gloria Steinmetz, sat at one of several tables with relatives and friends of Montgomerites, as Montgomery attendees were sometimes called. At a far end of the table, Frederick Chase sat not far from Crayton Warbler, their attention shyly on one another.

Dora and Missy were at a table with Charlie, Christine, C3, Sarah, and Livvie, where Christine had just finished a story about a startling argument that had broken out between a department commissioner and a council member at a city council meeting.

Charlie was shaking his head and laughing. "I'll tell you who should be running this city, no offense to my wife," he was saying. "Our granddaughter, Livvie! What they need to do over there is get over themselves and their little fights about policy and focus on kindness. And who's kinder than our Livvie? That's what our residents need, don't you think? Kindness!"

Christine smiled indulgently at her husband. She'd ceased trying to make him understand the details of running a city. She kept her husband on a long leash, making sure to keep an eye on his alcohol consumption and his enthusiastic attention toward some of his female clients. Charlie was a character who ran on emotion; he meant well—sometimes too well. What he needed was boundaries—quietly enforced boundaries—and a woman's love that was two parts wife and one part mother.

Dora and Missy looked happily at one another, glad to again be a part of their group of friends.

At the same table were Adam Geller and Thelma, the former hobbled by a recent accident and concerned about both his cancer and his upcoming hip replacement.

"What happened to you now?" Missy asked Adam, noting his elbow crutches, which were a new addition.

Thelma answered for her employer. "I'll tell you what he shouldn't have been doing. He shouldn't have been trying to use under-the-arm crutches on stairs." She shook her head. "Those are accidents waiting to happen. Whose fault is it you lost focus and took a step out into the air? Not mine!"

Missy looked horrified. Adam shrugged helplessly. He'd been asking a question of everyone at the table. He directed the question now to Dora. "And what do you love, young lady?"

Dora looked again at Missy, though she was thinking of her beloved Franny, who was gone several years now. She still missed Franny every day but chose to believe that her sweet girl could see her, and was happy that she'd again found love.

"I'll tell you what she loves," Thelma declared, in a voice that could be heard throughout the cafeteria, "and what Missy loves too!"

Dora shaded her eyes with a palm, afraid of what might come next.

"Dogs!" Thelma exclaimed. "If they're not tracking down criminals, they're out on the street, tracking down stray dogs and keeping them for themselves!"

Both Dora and Missy laughed. Though she was exaggerating, Thelma wasn't entirely wrong.

"But that's not all!" Thelma wasn't finished. "Dora loves beating the crap out of just about anyone, and Missy just relishes being the smartest one around. She's a librarian, she'll tell you, like that's some big deal."

Adam stood up, with the help of his new crutches. "Only one thing is more important than whatever it is we love—being able to let go of that thing. Being prepared to die, and to die well." He tapped the floor with his crutch for emphasis.

Thelma shot him a withering glare. "Well, aren't you the life of the party!" she brayed, "Mr. Obsessed-with-Death."

"I'll tell you what I love!" Missy had stood up and was doing a surprisingly good impression of Thelma's foghorn voice. "I just love telling you all about how ridiculous everyone is!"

No one spoke for a moment. Everyone looked at Thelma, who could be explosive and unpredictable.

But Thelma slapped her hand on the table and roared with laughter. "Good one, librarian!" she cried.

At the front of the room, Kelvin finished his song and cleared his throat into the microphone. "Ahem! Please give me your attention. At this time, I would like to introduce a guest performer who has been working hard on a number that he would like to dedicate to someone special. Okay, we're ready for you. Come on up."

Six-year-old Drew Burrell walked shyly up to the microphone. "Kelvin's been helping me practice a song I want to sing for my mom."

While Vanessa beamed at her son, at Kelvin, and at little Buster, who sat quietly in her lap, Drew sang "This Little Light of Mine" to his mother, who crouched next to him with his brother, Buster, in her arms.

THE END

• • •

In another section of Beach City, a different kind of group event was in full swing—the participants were singing in exuberant unison. They'd been meeting monthly for nearly a year, and each meeting was larger and more energized than the last. Their songs were about the happy, if imagined, days of old and the better days to come—days when people very much like themselves would fulfill their destinies, and again triumph over forces that wanted to dilute the purity and mastery of their blood. Unlike previous meetings, this gathering ended, not with attendees going home, but with the handing out of pamphlets to be spread among throngs of young people who were eager for something or someone powerful enough to earn their allegiance.

Look for Book 6 in David E. Feldman's
Dora Ellison Mystery Series: A Divisive Storm.

THE END

Dear Reader: Thanks so much for reading A Special Storm.
I hope you will join my mailing list to learn more about my next
books at:
https://www.davidefeldman.com/books.shtml

If you enjoyed this book, I would be grateful if you would
post a review online.
See you again soon!

-DF

www.ingramcontent.com/pod-product-compliance
Lightning Source LLC
Chambersburg PA
CBHW070458300726
48975CB00007B/2226